FREE WILLY 2

THE ADVENTURE HOME

BOOKS BY TODD STRASSER

Abe Lincoln for Class President
Help! I'm Trapped in the First Day of School
Please Don't *Be Mine, Julie Valentine*
Help! I'm Trapped in My Teacher's Body
The Diving Bell
The Lifeguards
Free Willy (novelization)
Home Alone™ (novelization)
Home Alone II™: Lost in New York (novelization)
The Mall from Outer Space

FREE WILLY 2

THE ADVENTURE HOME

A novelization by Todd Strasser
Based on the Motion Picture
Written by Karen Janszen and Corey Blechman and John Mattson
Based on Characters Created by Keith A. Walker

SCHOLASTIC INC.
New York Toronto London Auckland Sydney

ISBN 0-590-25227-5

12 11 10 9 8 7 6 5 4 3 5 6 7 8 9/9 0/0

Printed in the U.S.A. 40

First Scholastic printing, July 1995

To Sarah, David, and Flora Samis

1

The sky over the ocean was blue and dotted with cottony white clouds. The sun's rays shimmered on the cold clear waters below. Waves creased the ocean's surface. Beneath the waves, thick shafts of sunlight tunneled down into the dark depths. A high-pitched jabber of squeals and whistlelike calls pierced this liquid world. They told all who listened that a family of orcas was coming.

The mother, Catspaw, led the way. She was the largest and the strongest. Behind her followed her children, spouting, chattering, playing in the waves. First came Luna, named for the white crescent-shaped patch on her dorsal fin. She always stayed close to her mother's tail. And following them was a medium-sized male with three black spots on his throat, his dorsal fin curled sideways.

His name was Willy.

More than two years had passed since Jesse had

helped him escape from the adventure park aquarium. Now those years of captivity were just a distant memory. Like his fellow killer whales, he knew no boundaries. The vast Pacific ocean was his home.

He had just one problem . . . Littlespot, the youngest member of the family, named for the small, dark spot under his chin. Nothing was more annoying than a kid brother who wouldn't leave him alone even though it *was* great to be back with his family. But no matter where Willy went, Littlespot followed. If Willy leapt out of the water, Littlespot was right behind him. If Willy spyhopped, there was Littlespot, poking his head out of the water beside him.

The only way Willy could shake Littlespot was to dive into the dark cold depths, where the younger orca was afraid to follow. So Willy dove . . . down, down, down to where the deep blue waters finally blotted out the sun and the pressure was so strong it hurt his ears.

Somewhere between Willy and the surface, Littlespot lingered in the water, puzzled, unhappy, and afraid to go any deeper. Suddenly, everything went dark! Littlespot froze with fear. Looking up, he saw a huge dark shape churning through the waters above. It was enormous! Gigantic! Seized with terror, Littlespot squealed for help and raced blindly away.

Deep below, Willy heard both the churning propellers and his little brother's cry. Unlike Littlespot, Willy had seen these huge ships before and knew it wouldn't harm him. But Littlespot didn't know that. Instantly feeling protective, and forgetting how annoying his little brother could be, Willy raced upward.

He found Littlespot careening around in frantic circles of fear. Willy swam up and nudged him with his nose. Feeling his big brother nearby, Littlespot quickly calmed down. Together they swam out from under the shadow of the ship and rejoined Catspaw and Luna.

Moments later, the orcas were again frolicking in the waves while the huge oil tanker was just a dot on the horizon, steaming steadily toward Seattle. Neither the whales nor those on board the ship could possibly suspect that their paths would soon cross again . . . with tragic results.

2

Jesse sat behind the controls of Glen's boat, the *Little Dipper*. Jesse was fourteen now, taller, stronger, less wary of the world around him. His hair was still blond and shaggy, and he still lived with Glen and Annie Greenwood. That was probably the best thing that had ever happened to him. It was hard to believe that before they'd taken him in, he'd lived on the streets and stolen food to survive. Life was a lot better now that he didn't have to worry about where his next meal was coming from.

The *Little Dipper* was an old wooden boat that Glen had painstakingly restored. It had a white hull and a wooden center console for steering.

"What's this?" Jesse asked Glen, who was standing behind him in the boat, explaining how everything worked.

"The throttle," Glen said. "It has three positions. Push it ahead and you go forward. In the middle you're in neutral. Pull it back and you go in reverse."

Out of the corner of his eye, Jesse saw something in the distance. He quickly pulled a pair of binoculars off the console and pressed them to his eyes for a closer look.

"Come on, Jesse," Glen said. "Pay attention."

But Jesse had other things on his mind. He quickly put down the binoculars, grabbed the side of the boat, and vaulted over.

"Jesse!" Glen gasped.

But it was too late. Jesse had gone overboard. . . .

And landed in the Greenwoods' driveway. The boat was on a trailer hitched to the back of Glen's car.

Jesse walked slowly down the driveway, careful not to appear to be in a rush. The girls he'd seen in the binoculars were riding up the street on their bikes. They were three of the prettiest girls from his school.

"Hi, Jesse." The first girl stopped her bike in the street and smiled.

"Hey, what's up?" Jesse smiled back. In the past year his whole attitude toward girls had changed. Before that they'd basically been slightly different looking and smelling human beings who could fill in on a baseball team when you couldn't find enough guys. But recently they'd become something else completely. Now Jesse found girls attractive, alluring, and deeply puzzling.

"You coming to the beach tonight?" the same girl asked. "There's gonna be a big bonfire."

"Can't," Jesse said, playing it cool. "I have to pack for vacation. We're going up to San Juan Island."

She looked disappointed. "Too bad. See you when you get back."

"Yeah."

The girl started to ride away. Jesse smiled and waved. He was disappointed too, but he knew better than to show it. Besides, she would still be around when he got back from vacation. Jesse turned and headed back up the driveway. Suddenly he noticed a car parked at the curb. It must have arrived while he was talking to the girl. He recognized it immediately. It belonged to Dwight, the social worker who'd placed Jesse with the Greenwoods.

Jesse felt a slight chill of apprehension and quickened his step. It had been a while since Dwight had visited. Jesse didn't think he was scheduled to come again until around Thanksgiving.

A moment later, he pushed open the door of the house and went through the kitchen into the living room. Annie and Glen were sitting on the couch. Dwight was sitting in the easy chair.

"Hey, Dwight, how'd you sneak in?" Jesse

asked, giving him a high five and studying his face for a clue.

"You were busy," Dwight replied. He looked pretty glum.

Jesse felt the chill again. He'd had two good years with the Greenwoods. If the social worker had bad news, he didn't want to hear it.

"Yeah, well, I'm starving," Jesse said. "Guess all that boating made me hungry."

He hoped everyone would laugh, but they didn't. Jesse turned to Dwight. "Staying for dinner?"

Dwight shook his head. Now Jesse knew there'd be no avoiding it. "What's going on?"

"Maybe you should sit down," Annie said.

It was serious. Jesse felt his chest grow tight. He remained standing and looked at Dwight.

"I have bad news, Jesse," the social worker said. "We found your mother in New York City. I'm afraid she's passed away."

His mother? Found? Dead!

"No." His chest felt so tight that he couldn't breathe. He couldn't believe it. Not his mom!

"I can't tell you how sorry I am," Dwight said.

"It can't be." Jesse could feel the blood draining from his face. He couldn't accept this. Not his mother . . .

"Jesse . . ." Annie had tears in her eyes.

Jesse stepped backward, as if trying to get away from it. He'd always known he'd see his mother again. *He'd known it!* This couldn't be true. They were saying that he'd *never* see her now.

Jesse said the first thing that popped into his head. "I should have gone to look for her."

"She didn't want to be found," Dwight said.

But Dwight didn't know. No one knew. Jesse could feel a huge pain welling up inside him. "I should have tried to help her."

"There's nothing you could have done," Glen said.

"Yes," Jesse insisted.

"It's not too late to help her, Jesse," Dwight said.

"What?" Jesse stared at him, not understanding.

"She left somebody behind," Dwight said.

Jesse didn't get it. "Like who?"

"You have a brother," Dwight said. "Well, he's a half brother actually. He's eight years old."

A brother? The thought shocked Jesse.

"He was living with her. In New York."

The words ripped through Jesse's heart. How come his mom had kept this brother and not *him*?

"Forget it," Jesse said angrily. "I don't want a brother."

Everyone looked at him with shocked expressions on their faces. A fury swept through Jesse like a hurricane.

"But, Jesse . . ." Annie started to get up.

Don't you get it?" Jesse shouted at them. "I don't want some stupid brother! I want my mother back!"

Annie tried to put her arms around him, but Jesse pulled away and headed for the door. *Bang!* He slammed the door behind him and got out of the house. The next thing he knew, he was running, running . . . as if somehow, if he ran far enough, he could get away from it all.

3

He was sitting on the edge of a pier, looking down at the water. He'd run out of running room, and anyway, there was no place left to go. Tears were falling out of his eyes, making little splashes in the sea water a dozen feet below. His mother was gone. She'd always been gone, but now . . . she'd never come back. And she'd betrayed him. Everyone had said she couldn't take care of a kid. But she had. She'd had this other kid.

The wooden planks of the dock creaked behind him. Jesse turned and saw Glen coming. He wished Glen would leave him alone, but that was what was good *and* bad about the Greenwoods. They always came after him.

Glen sat down next to him on the pier. For a while neither said a word. But Jesse couldn't keep what he was feeling inside.

"How could she ditch me and then have another

kid?" he asked angrily. "How come she kept him and not me?"

"I don't know," Glen said.

Jesse felt the anger slowly start to drain away. He'd learned long ago that there was no point in asking questions where his mother was concerned. No one had the answers. A deep sadness washed through him. He felt his shoulders sag with hopelessness. The tears fell faster.

"I really thought I would see her again," he said with a sniff. "I thought if I was really good, I would get her back."

"Take it from me, Jesse," Glen reassured him. "You are really good."

If there was one person he could talk to, one person who wouldn't make fun of him, it was Glen. Jesse looked up at him and wiped his eyes. "What do I do? I always thought I'd see her again. Now Dwight says she's gone, but I can't let go of her."

"You don't have to let go of her," Glen said. "She's part of you. She'll always be part of you."

Jesse nodded. Until he'd met Glen and Annie, he'd never taken much stock in what grown-ups said. But Glen was always straight with him. He wanted to stop crying now, but the tears wouldn't stop falling. He turned away and stared down at the water.

"It's the cold air," he said. "It makes my eyes run."

"Yeah." Glen patted him softly on the back. "I get that, too."

Later, they walked back toward the house. Jesse's eyes were dry now.

"So, uh, Dwight had some more news," Glen said. "Your brother's coming tomorrow. He's going to stay with us for a couple of weeks."

"Huh?" Jesse gave him a look of disbelief. "From New York?"

"It's called Kinship Care," Glen explained. "It's actually the law, Jesse. You're his only known relative. He's supposed to stay with us until Dwight can place him with a family."

But Jesse already knew what might happen. "Or until Annie falls in love with him and never lets him leave."

Glen rolled his eyes. "Exactly."

Jesse shook his head. He didn't want that kid near him. "This stinks, Glen."

"Tell me about it," Glen said.

Jesse stared at him, puzzled for a second. Then he got it. He'd given Glen a really hard time when he'd first moved in. Running away, breaking windows . . . dumb stuff like that. Glen couldn't be looking forward to going through that again.

Then Jesse thought of something else. "What about our vacation?" he asked.

"What about it?" Glen asked.

"You want to bring him?" Jesse asked.

"Looks like we're gonna have to," Glen said. "Don't worry. You'll get to see Randolph. We'll still do everything we planned. It'll be fun."

Jesse studied him closely. "You really believe that?"

"Ask me in a couple of days," Glen replied with a wink.

4

Jesse stayed in bed the next night, listening to music and playing his guitar. After a while he heard the doorbell ring and knew Dwight had arrived. He could hear voices downstairs, but he couldn't hear what they were saying. A little while later Annie knocked on his door and came in.

"What's he look like?" Jesse asked.

"Different," Annie said. "Why don't you come downstairs and see for yourself."

"Don't feel like it," Jesse replied with a shrug.

"Why don't you talk to him?" Annie asked. "Maybe you could learn something."

Learn something from an eight year old? Jesse gave Annie a funny look. "Like what?"

"He's been living with your mom for the last eight years," Annie said. "You tell me."

She had a point. Jesse got off his bed and went downstairs. Jesse's half brother was sitting at the kitchen table with Dwight while Annie and Glen busied themselves in the kitchen. It sort of reminded Jesse of the scene when he first arrived at the Greenwoods'.

Jesse focused more closely on the kid. He had shaggy brown hair. He was wearing an army fatigue jacket, baggy jeans, and black boots. He wore a Knicks cap backwards. Jesse stepped into the kitchen. Without looking too interested, he said, "Hi."

"Whatever," the kid said with a shrug and tried to look uninterested.

Jesse couldn't help being a little amused. It was sort of funny that this eight-year-old twerp was trying to out-cool him. But he kept his guard up. It was important to establish who was cooler.

"Jesse, meet Elvis," Annie said.

"Elvis?" Jesse repeated in disbelief.

The kid ignored that and looked at Glen. "So, are you guys rich? Dwight said you were rich."

"Now, Elvis, I never said that," Dwight replied.

"I told Dwight I could only stay with people who were loaded," Elvis informed them. "So it wouldn't be too much of an adjustment."

"I didn't say that, either," Dwight said.

Annie, Glen, and Jessie exchanged looks. Who did this kid think he was kidding?

"Well, Elvis, I guess that's going to be one of life's little disappointments," Glen said.

* * *

The next morning, Elvis stood in the doorway and watched while Jesse helped Glen and Annie lug the suitcases and backpacks out to the car. Jesse could have been annoyed, but he forgave the kid for not volunteering to help. After all, he was still brand-new here.

As they got into the car, Jesse and Elvis glared at each other.

Then Jesse shook his head and stared out the window while Glen backed the car and boat trailer out of the driveway. It was hard to believe that this kid and he had come from the same mother. Then Jesse remembered what he was like at eight. Maybe it wasn't so hard to believe.

Soon they were headed north in the car, pulling the *Little Dipper* on the trailer behind them. Elvis just stared out the window. After a while, Annie turned around from the front seat and tried to get him to talk.

"So, Elvis," she said. "How'd you get the name Elvis?"

"My mom," Elvis replied. His tone said he thought it was a stupid question.

Glen looked at him in the rearview mirror. "Hey, that's how I got my name, too."

"Whatever," Elvis said. "I'm going to be a big movie star, just like my dad."

"Right," Jesse said. *That* was a good one.

"My dad's Al Pacino," Elvis said.

Jesse sighed. Did this kid really think they believed that stuff?

Now Elvis turned to Jesse. "My friends call me the Godfather."

"You have friends?" Jesse asked, to make sure the kid knew he wasn't fooling anyone.

"Fans," Elvis corrected him.

"Give me a break," Jesse groaned. This kid wasn't like him when he was eight. He was a million times worse. In the front seat, Annie and Glen shared a look, like they couldn't believe him either.

Pretty soon the road they were on started to wind its way along the coast. Suddenly Elvis practically climbed over Jesse to point out the window.

"Hey, the ocean!" he cried, momentarily forgetting to be cool.

"So?" Jesse said, pushing him off.

"My mom loved the ocean," Elvis said.

Jesse glanced at him, wondering about that. Was it true?

"She was born at sea, you know," Elvis said.

"That's interesting," Annie said, looking over the front seat at him. Jesse was also interested. He'd never known anything about her background.

"On an aircraft carrier," Elvis said. "Nobody's supposed to know that. It's classified."

A cloud of disappointment settled over Jesse. For a second there, he thought the kid was telling the truth, but it was just another Elvis story. Jesse was really getting tired of them.

"Do you come with remote?" he snapped, wishing he could hit a button and turn him off.

Later that day they drove onto the ferry that would take them over to San Juan Island. Everyone got out of their cars and stood at the ferry's railing, taking in the crystal blue waters, pine-tree covered islands, and the snowcapped mountain peaks in the distance. In between the islands, fishing trawlers moved slowly along with flocks of squawking seagulls hovering over them like mosquitos.

Jesse and Elvis stood at the railing near the stern of the ferry. Elvis, of course, was working hard to keep a bored expression on his face. Half the time Jesse thought he was a jerk, but the other half of the time he couldn't help being curious about him. Jesse had carried so many questions about his mother for so long. And Elvis must have some of the answers. Jesse found himself looking at the kid, wanting to know him better. Suddenly Elvis turned and caught him.

"What are you staring at?" he asked.

"What are *you* staring at?" Jesse shot back defensively.

Elvis shrugged. "A bunch of water."

Elvis pointed at an island they were passing. A large wooden structure stood near the shore and a group of people were standing on it. "Do they have an amusement park on this island?"

"No, they have a whale-spotting station."

"You mean where they paint spots on whales?" Elvis asked.

Jesse rolled his eyes. The kid acted so smart about some stuff, and so dumb about other stuff. Just then a commotion broke out at the stern. Everyone was pressing toward the railing and pointing. Jesse moved back and joined them. A pod of black and white orcas was surfing and playing in the ferry's wake.

Jesse looked carefully, but Willy wasn't among them. He felt a wistful pang inside. More than two years had passed since he'd seen his friend. He often wondered if he'd ever see him again.

5

The ferry docked in a harbor, near a small seaside town with a boat marina and a main street lined with old buildings. The Greenwoods got back into their car and drove off the ferry and through town. From there they drove along the coast of San Juan Island until they came to the campground where they'd spend their vacation.

The campground was located on the side of a hill overlooking the ocean straits, the body of water that ran from the Pacific ocean through the islands between the state of Washington and the Island of Vancouver. There were picnic tables and barbecue pits spread around the grounds.

They set up two tents. A large one for Annie and Glen, and a smaller one for Jesse and Elvis. Once again, Elvis sat and watched while the others worked. That bothered Jesse, but he had other things on his mind. As he helped Glen put up the tents, he kept looking down the dirt road that wound through the campground.

Finally, a light-colored pickup bounced up the road. Jesse recognized it immediately.

"Randolph!" he shouted and started to run toward the truck.

Randolph was the former caretaker at the amusement park where Willy had been confined. He had helped Jesse free Willy. Randolph was a Haida Indian and had taught Jesse the story of Natselane, the Indian brave who, according to ancient legend, had brought orcas into the world. Now Randolph worked at Orca Institute, an organization that studied and protected the killer whales.

Randolph got out of the pickup and he and Jesse shared a bear hug. "Hey, Jess, look at you! You must've grown six inches."

"Four and a half," Jesse said.

"Since breakfast," Glen added as he came up behind them.

Randolph greeted Glen and Annie warmly. Then he nodded at Elvis. "Is this the brother I've heard about?"

Jesse's half brother shook Randolph's hand. "The name's Elvis. I'm half Apache."

Jesse saw a smile creep across Randolph's face. "Pleased to meet you, Elvis. The Apache are the sworn enemy of my people."

Elvis's eyes went wide. "Really?"

"No," Randolph said with a big grin. "Just kidding." Then he turned to Jesse. "Come on, we're going for a ride."

"Where?" Jesse asked.

"To do some whale spotting." Randolph climbed back into the pickup and Jesse went around to the passenger side. Elvis was following him, but he'd had enough of that kid for now. He climbed in and slammed the door, leaving Elvis behind.

Randolph put the truck in gear and they bounced down the bumpy dirt road. As he drove, Randolph sifted through a leather bag on the front seat. He pulled out a small, primitively carved wooden orca on a string necklace.

"This is for you," he said, handing it to Jesse. "From my village."

"Wow!" Jesse held the carving up and studied it. Sunlight reflected off the wood-carved whale. Randolph reached across and tapped Jesse on the chest with his fingers.

"My people believe your soul lives here," he said. "When you wear the necklace around your neck, the orca is close to your spirit."

"This is great! Thanks." Jesse put the necklace on. The carved orca rested over his chest.

"I've missed having you around," Randolph said as they drove. "I don't know many people who have what you have."

Jesse wasn't sure what Randolph meant. "What do I have?"

"Medicine roots. It makes you special."

There was a time when Jesse might have scoffed at that. But that was years ago, before Willy. They rode along in silence for a moment.

"Setting Willy free was the best thing I ever did," Randolph said.

"Me, too. The best." Jesse nodded and gazed out the window. Down through the trees he caught glimpses of the blue waters that lapped against the island's shores. He missed Willy. "Have you seen him?"

"Willy?" Randolph shook his head. "No."

They turned down a narrow gravel road and passed a painted wood sign that said ORCA INSTITUTE. After Randolph quit the amusement park, he went to work here, studying and protecting the killer whales. The institute was housed in a log building that was too large to call a cabin. Past the building was a long dock. Moored there was a thirty-foot cabin cruiser called the *Natselane* after the Indian warrior from the myth. Randolph parked the truck by the dock.

"Where're we going?" Jesse asked.

"Out on the boat."

"Cool." Jesse walked out on the dock and climbed onto the deck of the *Natselane*. Randolph climbed up to the bridge above the cabin and started the engines.

"Take up the stern line and we'll be off," he shouted.

"You talkin' to me?" Jesse asked.

"Her." Randolph pointed toward the stern.

Jesse turned and saw a girl come out on the deck. She was slender and tall. She wore a T-shirt and cutoffs, and her long brown hair was tucked up under a baseball cap. Some tall girls Jesse knew walked around hunched over, as if embarrassed by their height. But she stood tall and proud. She was really pretty. Jesse couldn't help staring at her.

"Ahem." Randolph cleared his throat.

Jesse looked up at him. "Aren't you gonna introduce me?"

"No," Randolph replied. "I want you up here with me. I might even let you steer."

Jesse climbed up on the bridge and joined Randolph. The bright sunlight sparkling on the water made him squint. "Who is she?"

"My orca spotter," Randolph replied tersely. He had that Papa-bear tone, like he didn't want Jesse to go near her. But Jesse kept looking back as the girl coiled the stern line into a neat circle on the aft deck.

Without warning, Randolph shoved a pair of binoculars into Jesse's hands. He pointed out into the strait. "Here, keep your eyes peeled for whales."

Jesse scanned the water. But, as if the binoculars had a mind of their own, they swept around toward the stern of the boat and focused on the girl. Now he could see her more closely. She had an upturned nose and high cheekbones. She was beautiful.

"Hey." Randolph nudged him with his elbow and pointed out over the bow. "Give me a break, she's my goddaughter. I look out for her." Then he looked back at the stern and shouted, "Nadine!"

Jesse suddenly felt nervous. He held his breath as she climbed up to the bridge. Randolph introduced them.

"Hi," Jesse said, trying not to sound too eager.

"Hello." She studied him in a reserved manner.

"Would you take the wheel, Nadine?" Randolph said. "I want to take Jesse below and show him the setup."

Nadine took the wheel while Randolph and Jesse went down into the cabin. It was filled with electronic equipment, monitors, sonar screens, tape recorders, everything you'd need to study whales. Randolph flipped some switches on a tape recorder and the reels began to turn slowly.

"Listen to this," he said. The high-pitched squeals and whistles of whales started to come through the speakers. "We've been tracking this pod all the way up the Pacific coast."

He fiddled with the knobs some more, and the sounds became clearer. "Each pod has its own distinct dialect, like an accent. It helps us identify them from a distance."

Randolph kept adjusting the knobs on the tape

recorder, slowly filtering out the background sounds until one whale call remained. Suddenly Jesse felt a shiver. He got light-headed for a moment. No, it couldn't be. . . . He gave Randolph a questioning look.

"I didn't want to tell you until I knew for sure," Randolph said. "But we're pretty sure Willy's pod has been in these waters for a couple of days."

"We have to find him!" Jesse gasped.

"That's why I brought you here." Randolph patted him on the shoulder. "But I have to warn you. Willy's been living in the wild, in the open sea, for the past two years. There's no telling if he'll remember us."

"He'll remember me." Jesse was convinced.

"There's no telling how tame he'll be," Randolph warned. "There are no guarantees."

"But we have to try," Jesse insisted.

Randolph nodded. "Sure, we've got nothing to lose."

They rejoined Nadine on the bridge. Randolph took the wheel and Nadine slipped on a pair of headphones. Jesse gave her a curious look.

"They're hydrophones," she explained. "To listen for the whales."

Randolph pointed off to the right and Jesse saw a group of dolphins playing in the waves.

"White-sided dolphins," Randolph said. "The lucky ones."

"The unlucky ones are in aquariums all over the

country," Nadine said. "Their normal life span in the wild can reach twenty-five years. But in captivity, they won't live past the age of four."

Just then, Randolph cut the engines. The boat rose under the backwash and began to drift. He flicked a switch that let the hydrophone sounds come out through a speaker on the bridge. Jesse could hear a distant rumbling sound like engines, along with some squeals and squeaks.

"The rumbling sound means there's a tanker out there somewhere," Randolph said.

"Any orcas?" Jesse asked.

Randolph listened for a moment, then shook his head and started up the engines again. "Not here. Let's try Capital Point. Maybe they're having lunch."

While Randolph steered, Jesse and Nadine stood near each other, taking turns with the binoculars. After a while, Jesse put the glasses down and glanced at her. Nadine turned and glanced at him. She had a playful glint in her eye.

"So . . ." Jesse wanted to say something, but he couldn't think of what.

"Buttons on ice cream, see if they stick," Nadine said.

"Huh?" Jesse didn't get it.

"Sew buttons on ice cream, see if they stick," Nadine said again. "It's an expression. Somebody says, 'so,' and you say — "

"Buttons on ice cream, see if they stick." Jesse grinned. "That's pretty good."

Nadine smiled back. "Yeah."

The boat lurched around in a sudden turn and both Jesse and Nadine looked up to Randolph, who was pointing. In the distance, Jesse saw two whales breach and spout.

"J-pod," Randolph said. "Willy's family is usually with them."

"Let's get closer!" Jesse said excitedly, pressing against the rail to see. He counted at least half a dozen whales, diving and surfacing.

"Can't," Randolph replied. "We're required by law to stay a hundred yards away."

A huge orca surfaced, its mammoth tail flapping out of the water.

"That's Catspaw," Randolph said. "Willy's mother."

Willy's mother! Jesse felt a rush of excitement.

"Look over there!" Nadine pointed off to the right, where three other orcas surfaced and dove. One was medium-sized, the others were small and young.

"Was that them?" Jesse asked.

"Too far away to tell," Randolph said. "One looked about Willy's size. The other two were smaller. Could have been his brother and sister, Littlespot and Luna."

"He's got a brother and sister?" Jesse asked in amazement.

Randolph smiled. "Yup."

Jesse picked up the binoculars and peered through them. A small orca surfaced again. "That one's got a white patch on his fin."

"*Her* fin," Randolph corrected him. "That's Luna, Willy's sister."

Jesse kept the binoculars pressed against his eyes. If Luna was there . . . Suddenly a larger orca broke through the surface. Unlike the others, its dorsal fin curled sideways. That could only mean one thing!

"Willy!" Jesse shouted. "It's him!"

6

"Willy!" Jesse called to the orca. Willy and the other orcas kept moving.

The whales changed direction and headed toward the open ocean, picking up speed, moving away now.

Randolph slowed the boat.

"What are you doing?" Jesse gasped.

"It's getting late," Nadine said. "We have a long way back."

"They're hunting now," Randolph said as he turned the boat around. "We can try again tomorrow."

Jesse felt an acute mixture of joy and disappointment. Joy that he'd seen his old friend, and disappointment that Willy had swum away without recognizing him or letting him get a closer look. Was Randolph right? Had Willy forgotten him? He stood beside Randolph and Nadine as they headed back toward the Orca Institute.

"Why's Willy's fin still bent?" he asked.

"The cartilage grew that way when he was in captivity," Nadine said. "Now it'll never change."

"At least it makes him easy to recognize," Randolph added.

Nadine went below. Jesse stood with Randolph for a while, then went below too. He found her in the cabin, writing in a notebook.

"So, uh, what are you doing?" he asked, still feeling nervous around her.

"We keep a log of whale sightings," Nadine explained without looking up.

"How long have you worked for Randolph?" Jesse asked.

"Since he got here," Nadine said. "The last two summers."

"He said something about being your godfather?"

"Yes," Nadine said. "I've known him ever since I can remember. His dad and my dad were in the army together."

She closed the notebook and left the cabin. Jesse followed her out to the stern deck. They both stood at the rear of the boat, staring out past the ship's wake, back toward the horizon where they'd last seen Willy. The sun was starting to go down and the water was turning dark. The air felt cooler. Nadine hugged herself.

"I worked with Randolph for a summer," Jesse said.

"I know," replied Nadine.

"He told you?"

"Uh-huh."

Jesse realized he felt a little jealous. He used to work with Randolph, now Nadine did. Like he was part of the past or something.

"Did Randolph ever tell you that I have medicine roots?" Jesse asked.

Nadine gave him a funny look. "Let's see 'em."

"It's not something you carry on you," Jesse explained. "It's something inside you."

Nadine's eyebrows rose slightly. "Am I supposed to be impressed?"

"Yeah." Jesse said. "I mean . . . well, are you?"

Nadine just rolled her eyes. Jesse felt a little dumb. Maybe it was better if he kept quiet.

7

They got back to the Orca Institute, and then Randolph drove Jesse back to the campground. All Jesse could think about was going back out on the boat the next day to look for Willy again. Randolph stopped the pickup. Jesse saw Glen sitting alone on a log by a campfire.

"Set your alarm clock early, Jess," Randolph said. "We'll go out at dawn."

"I'll be ready," Jesse said, reaching for the car door. Then he stopped and looked back. "You think he'll remember me, don't you?"

Randolph looked back at him and didn't reply for a moment. Then he took a deep breath. "I hope so, Jess."

Jesse knew Randolph would never promise him something that might not be true. "Well, this was really great. Thanks."

Randolph smiled. "My pleasure, Jess."

Jesse got out and walked over to the fire. Glen

looked up. The light of the orange flames flickered on his face. "How'd it go?"

"We found Willy," Jesse said, sitting down on the log. He gazed at the dancing flames and felt the heat of the fire on his face. "It was so cool. I mean, I only saw him for a second, a million miles away, with binoculars."

"That's pretty good," Glen said. "Considering it's been a long time since you've seen him."

Jesse pictured Willy in his mind, following Catspaw and frolicking in the waves with Luna and Littlespot. "It must be great for him."

"To be with his family, you mean?"

"Yeah." Jesse just kept staring into the fire. He still wondered why Willy hadn't responded to his call. Maybe he'd been too far away to hear.

"You think he misses me?" he asked.

"When you're in someone's heart, you stay there forever," Glen said.

Two silhouettes appeared at the edge of the campfire light and came closer. As the flames lit them, Jesse saw that it was Annie and Elvis. Wow, he'd been so preoccupied with Willy that he'd almost forgotten about that kid.

"Time to go to sleep, boys," Annie said, kneeling down and lighting a kerosene lamp. "Come on, Jesse, let's get the tent ready."

They went inside the smaller tent and laid out the foam pads and sleeping bags side by side. As usual, Elvis stood and watched.

"All ready," Annie said, patting Elvis's sleeping bag.

Elvis didn't budge. "I can't sleep on the ground."

"We're all sleeping on the ground," Jesse said. "We're camping."

Elvis pointed at the sleeping bags. "How come you have two foam pads and I only have one?"

"We were all supposed to have two," Jesse said. "But no one knew you were coming."

"I have a bad back," Elvis said.

Jesse just stared at him. The kid was unreal!

"Jesse, why don't you let Elvis have the extra pad?" Annie asked. "He's our guest, after all."

Jesse grudgingly let Elvis have the extra pad. With a smug look on his face, Elvis rolled back his sleeping bag and stuck the pad underneath. Annie left and they both got into their sleeping bags. Jeese turned down the kerosene lamp until it was dark.

"You don't have a bad back," he said.

"Do so," Elvis replied. "I have spasms. Ever since I went bungee jumping in the Alps."

Jesse rolled his eyes in disbelief. This kid was so full of it, he wanted to scream. He sat up in his sleeping bag and traced an imaginary line between them down the center of the tent.

"See this line?" he asked.

"No," said Elvis.

"Cross it and I'll kill you," Jesse said ominously.

He laid back down in the dark and closed his eyes. He just wanted to go to sleep and get up in the morning and find Willy.

"Glen and Annie told me all about you and Willy," Elvis said.

"Go to sleep," Jesse said.

"Same exact thing happened to me two summers ago," said Elvis.

"Shut up!" Jesse snapped. The kid was like a gnat buzzing around your head that you couldn't get rid of. A total pain.

In the dark, Jesse heard Elvis's sleeping bag rustle. "Is *this* the line you don't want me to cross?"

"You're dead," Jesse muttered.

"Or is *this* the line?" Elvis taunted him.

That was it. If Jesse spent one more second in that tent he would strangle the kid. He threw back the sleeping bag, yanked on his shoes, and stormed out. Outside, Glen was still sitting by the fire.

"Hey, where're you going?" he asked, surprised.

"Out of here," Jesse grumbled, and stomped off into the woods.

He walked down through the trees toward the shore. A bait dock stuck out into the moonlit water and he walked out to the end of it and sat down with his feet hanging over the edge. It was quiet. The moonlight glimmered like a million little ripples on the water's surface. Jesse was glad to be alone.

He pulled his harmonica out of his pocket and played a slow, mournful tune. Then, as he tried to put the harmonica back in his pocket, his hand slipped and the harmonica landed with a *plop!* in the dark water below.

"Great," Jesse muttered. First Elvis, now his harmonica. He leaned over and looked down into the black water as if he might be able to see it somehow.

KER-SPLASH! The next thing Jesse knew, a huge gusher of water rose up and soaked him right through to the skin.

Plap! Jesse quickly wiped the water out of his eyes and looked down. A huge black shape with a white throat was staring back at him, with his harmonica on its tongue.

"Willy!" he cried. He couldn't believe it! Willy was there! Right before his eyes! He must've heard the harmonica!

Willy chattered happily at him, spyhopping and circling slowly, the way he used to when he wanted Jesse to swim with him.

"Come here, Willy." Jesse kneeled at the edge of the dock and waved excitedly at him. "Over here."

Willy came close and stuck his head out of the water. Jesse stroked his cold, wet skin. He'd forgotten how large orcas grew. Willy was about one and a half times as long as the *Little Dipper*.

"Wow, you've grown," Jesse said happily. "I guess you've been eating pretty well out here, huh?"

He gave Willy the "mouth open" signal and the big killer whale instantly opened his mouth, revealing his pointed ivory-colored teeth, great pink tongue, . . . and Jesse's harmonica. "Wow, you found it!" Jesse said as he removed the instrument from the orca's mouth. "Thanks, boy." Jesse rubbed his tongue. Willy always loved that. He still couldn't believe his friend was back. He *knew* Willy wouldn't forget him!

"I missed you, boy," Jesse said, feeling overcome with emotion. Suddenly the things he'd been keeping inside began to bubble up to the surface. Jesse felt his spirits suddenly shift from happy to sad.

"You know, I lost my mom," he said.

As if sensing the change in his friend, Willy let out a little wail of sympathy.

"You have your family again," Jesse said. "It must feel great. Without my mom, I feel like I'm nobody. Like I'm all alone."

Willy chattered happily.

"Yeah, yeah." Jesse grinned. "You always did know how to cheer me up."

Then a distant call came across the water. It was an orca call. Jesse peered out into the strait, but couldn't see anything. He knew, though, who was calling. "That's your mom, right?"

Willy rolled onto his side and waved at Jesse by flapping his fluke, the flipper that extended from his side. Then he turned and disappeared beneath the surface.

Jesse stood up on the dock. He was filled with excitement. Willy was here! He'd come back!

Jesse walked quickly down the dock and back through the woods. Ahead through the trees, he could see the campfire. Glen and Annie were sitting there, curled up together, watching the flames. Jesse couldn't wait to tell them the news.

"Hey, guys!" He stood there with a big grin on his face.

Annie turned to Glen and frowned. "Oh, yeah, Glen, he *really* looks upset."

"He really does miss me," Jesse said.

Glen and Annie looked at each other. Then they looked back at Jesse.

Jesse shined the flashlight in Glen's eyes. "Glen, he really *did* miss me!"

8

The good news was that he'd found Willy again. The bad news was that he had to go back into the tent and sleep next to that pathological liar, Elvis. That night Jesse lay in the tent with the kerosene lamp barely glowing. He was so consumed with excitement about seeing Willy again that he couldn't sleep.

Elvis lay still in the sleeping bag beside him. Soon Jesse's thoughts drifted toward the kid. He couldn't help it. Willy had found *his* mother. Jesse knew he'd never find his. So this kid was as close as he'd come.

Finally curiosity got the better of him. Jesse took the flashlight and held it closer to Elvis's face, as if searching for something that would tell him about his brother. In the lantern light the kid looked so young. Maybe Jesse couldn't blame him for trying to talk so big. He was just trying to make a place for himself in a world that didn't seem to have much room for him.

Suddenly, Elvis's eyes burst open. Jesse jerked back.

Elvis grinned. "Caught you."

Jesse turned the lantern off and rolled over.

"I never sleep," Elvis said behind him.

In the dark, Jesse clenched his fists. He really wanted to kill that kid.

The next time Jesse opened his eyes, it was light out. It was quiet and the air was damp and chilly, so he knew it was early morning. Jesse unzipped his sleeping bag and pulled his clothes inside to warm them up before he put them on. He got dressed in the sleeping bag and pulled on his baseball cap, then he left the tent. Mr. "I never sleep" was out like a light.

Outside a mist hung in the air and it was very quiet. No one else in the campground was out of their tents yet. Jesse stuck his head in Glen's and Annie's tent. They were both fast asleep.

"Glen, Annie," he whispered. "Wake up."

"Huh?" Glen slowly opened his eyes. "Wha . . . ?"

"It's morning," Jesse said. "C'mon, let's go out on the boat with Randolph."

"You want to lower your voice?" Glen asked with a yawn. "You'll wake the bears."

Now Annie opened her eyes. "Don't you usually get up at noon?"

"Randolph leaves at dawn," Jesse said. "It's dawn."

"Well, you go ahead, Jesse," Glen said. He

rolled over. Jesse started to leave.

"Hey, Jess?" Annie said.

"Yeah?"

"Take Elvis."

"Do I have to?"

"Yes."

Jesse trudged back to his tent and stuck his head in. "Hey!" he said in a loud voice. "Wake up!"

Elvis opened his eyes, startled. "What?"

"I'm goin' out on the boat," Jesse said. "Want to come?'

"Okay, yeah." Elvis crawled out of his sleeping bag and pulled on his cold clothes. Jesse wasn't about to share his camping tricks with this kid.

A few moments later they were walking up the hill. Elvis was lagging behind.

"Hurry up," Jesse called over his shoulder.

"I'm walking as fast as I can," Elvis said.

"Try running."

"I can't help it if my legs are shorter than yours," Elvis said.

Jesse slowed a little. "If Randolph leaves without us, I'll kill you."

"I have a black belt in karate," Elvis said.

"Yeah, well, I shoot laser death rays out of my eyes," Jesse fired back.

"Liar," Elvis said.

"Look who's talking," said Jesse.

They got down to the dock where the *Natselane*

was tied up. Jesse climbed onboard, followed by Elvis. They were heading for the cabin when Nadine came out and practically bumped into Jesse.

"Oh, hi." Jesse was a little flustered.

Nadine just nodded at him and moved on. Jesse stopped and watched her. Then he realized Elvis was staring at him.

Jesse turned and glared at the kid. "What?"

"Girls are the enemy," Elvis said.

"No, *you're* the enemy," Jess said and started to walk away.

"All girls have cooties from the galaxy Andromeda," Elvis yelled after hm.

Jesse found Randolph in the stern of the boat. He'd pulled open a wooden hatch and was working on something below the deck.

"Hey, Jesse," he said. "I'm afraid we've got a problem with the bilge pump."

"How big a problem?" Jesse asked, wondering how long it would be until they could go look for Willy again.

"Hard to say," Randolph said. "Could be a couple of hours. Could be a couple of days."

A cloud of disappointment covered Jesse's face.

"I'm sorry," Randolph said.

Near the cabin, Nadine was putting her notebook in a day pack.

Randolph didn't know that Jesse had seen Willy the night before, and Jesse didn't have time to tell him about it because it looked like Nadine was going to take off. Jesse figured if he couldn't see Willy today . . .

"See you later," Jesse said to Randolph.

"I'll let you know when it's fixed," Randolph said.

"Great."

Nadine got off the boat and started down the dock. Jesse followed a safe distance behind.

"Hey, where're you going?" a voice asked. Jesse stopped and turned. It was Elvis.

"Go back to camp," Jesse said. "Tell Glen and Annie I went out on the boat with Randolph. You couldn't go because you get seasick."

"But that would be a lie," Elvis said.

"I'm sure you can handle it," Jesse said. Then he turned and started to follow Nadine again.

"Where are you going?" Elvis called after him.

"None of your business," Jesse replied.

9

Jesse headed after Nadine, while Elvis followed at a safe distance. For a while she walked along a trail parallel to the shore. Then she cut down through the woods and disappeared.

Jesse quickened his step and came to a clearing. Before him lay a cove of still water, surrounded on three sides by a rocky shoreline. On the fourth side the cove opened into the wide, blue waters of the straits. A short boat dock and a small wooden swimming platform floated off one side of the cove. A longer boat dock stretched out from the other side. A bald eagle circled in the air high above. Between the cliffs and the water was a rocky beach dotted with driftwood, boulders and strands of seaweed.

Nadine was sitting on a log at the shore of the cove, staring out of the cove toward the vast blue straits. She seemed to be craning her neck to see something he couldn't see. Jesse moved closer.

Suddenly he saw what she was looking at! A

pod of orcas frolicking in the shallow water, surfacing and diving and playing tag. Jesse stared at them, mesmerized. Wait! Did one of them have a curved dorsal fin? Yes! It was Willy! This was his pod!

Forgetting for the moment about Nadine, Jesse scrambled forward to get a better look. He left the knoll and scrambled down a short rocky cliff to the shore.

Ooops! He slipped on a rock.

Splash! Jesse fell butt first into a small tidal pool.

Nadine stood up and saw him. She looked a little angry as she came down toward him.

"What do you think you're doing?" she asked.

"Sitting in the ocean," Jesse said, sitting in the tidal pool.

"You followed me, didn't you?" she said, accusingly.

"So?" Jesse shrugged.

Nadine seemed to soften slightly. She held out her hand and Jesse grabbed it. She pulled, helping him up.

Jesse waved his arm around. "What is this place?"

"My favorite place on earth," Nadine said, climbing the rocks back toward the shoreline.

Jesse followed her back to the shoreline, and sat down. Nadine didn't sit.

"I came here to be alone," she said.

"We're alone," Jesse said, not really catching her drift. About fifty yards out in the water, one of the whales spyhopped.

"Hey, look at that," Jesse said.

One after another, the whales spyhopped, looking like large black and white buoys poking out of the water. Nadine sat down beside Jesse and watched.

"Do they come here a lot?" Jesse asked.

"Yes, this is called Rubbing Beach," Nadine said. "Orcas come from all over to rub themselves on the bottom. Sometimes, if you sit here long enough, one of them will come really close."

"How close?" Jesse asked.

"One once came about ten feet away," Nadine said.

Jesse smiled. "You call that close?"

Nadine gave him a look. "These are wild killer whales. They're not pets, not amusement park rides. They don't like humans."

"Come with me," Jesse said. "I want to show you something." He pulled his harmonica out of his pocket and started to play. Nadine looked at him as if he were crazy.

"Are you still trying to impress me?" she asked.

"Yeah." Jesse kept playing. He was going to impress her, all right, but not with his harmonica playing.

Out in the water, one of the orcas left the pod and started to swim toward the cove. Jesse got up and scampered over the rocks. Nadine followed.

Finally Jesse kneeled down at the edge of the rocks and held his hand out. Willy popped up right in front of him and Jesse stroked his head.

"Hey, open up for a rubdown," Jesse said, giving the signal. Out of the corner of his eye, he saw Nadine watching them with an amazed look on her face.

Willy opened his mouth and Jesse rubbed his big pink tongue. Suddenly a second, smaller orca poked his head out of the water and opened his mouth.

"Hey, this must be your little brother," Jesse said. He reached over and tried to rub Littlespot's tongue, but the smaller whale quickly ducked under.

Jesse leaned toward Willy. "Hey, help me out here. I want to introduce you to somebody."

Willy nodded. Jesse turned back and waved to Nadine. "Come meet Willy."

On the dock behind him, Nadine hesitated. "Uh, I don't know."

Jesse turned back to Willy. "Willy, this is Nadine. Nadine, meet Willy. Give her a wave and show her how friendly you are."

Jesse gave Willy the signal. The orca rolled onto his side, raised his fluke and flapped it against the water.

Nadine laughed. "Okay, I'm impressed."

Willy swam back to Jesse and caught him by surprise, blowing his baseball cap off his head with his blowhole.

"Hey!" Jesse shouted playfully. "No fair!"

He got up and dove into the cove. The water was chilly, but he quickly got used to it. Willy circled around Jesse, then swam close and rubbed up against him. Jesse waved back to Nadine.

"Come on in, the water's fine!" he shouted.

Nadine stayed on the dock, looking apprehensive. "Get a grip, Jesse. That's a killer whale."

"Naw, he's a friend of mine," Jesse yelled back. Willy swam under Jesse and rose up. Jesse grabbed his dorsal fin and rode him in a big circle around the cove and into the shore. Nadine scurried along the rocks, trying to keep up. Her expression said she couldn't believe what she was seeing.

Finally, Willy dropped Jesse off near the shore and headed back out toward the pod. Jesse climbed out of the water. They stood together and watched as Willy's pod started to swim away.

"That was amazing," Nadine said. "I can't believe he let you do that."

Jesse turned and looked right into Nadine's eyes. She looked right back at him. He could feel goose bumps rise on his skin.

"I think he likes it," he said.

"I think you're right," Nadine said with a smile.

* * *

They spent the rest of the day together, walking along the shore, watching the otters float on their backs and eat fish, and the seals play. After a while, they found themselves standing on some rocks directly below the campground. Nadine had the binoculars and was watching something. Jesse sat slightly behind her, looking at how pretty she was. She was watching two seals playing in the water.

"You see that?" Nadine asked, still watching through the binoculars.

"Uh-huh," Jesse said, although he really hadn't seen anything.

"You don't see that every day," Nadine said.

"Nope," Jesse said. He still hadn't taken his eyes off her. You didn't see a girl like Nadine every day either.

"Uh oh." Nadine was looking at something else. Jesse looked up. You didn't need binoculars to see the huge long ship chugging past, belching black smoke from its smokestack. It was mostly flat and must have been the length of a couple of football fields. It's sides were stained with large brown patches of rust.

"That thing's huge," Jesse said. "What is it?"

"Oil tanker."

"Kind of ruins the view," Jesse said.

"Tell me about it," Nadine said. "They always come through here like it's their own private highway."

Jesse took the binoculars and stared through them. "How come it's so low in the water?"

"That's how they look when they're full of oil," Nadine said. "A ship that big can carry thousands of gallons of crude."

"Crude?" Jesse repeated uncertainly.

"Raw, unprocessed oil," Nadine explained. "It's totally toxic to all living things."

They heard someone coming through the woods behind them. It was Glen.

"Hey, Glen." Jesse waved.

"Hi." Glen waved back.

"Glen, this is Nadine," Jesse said. "She's Randolph's goddaughter."

"Nice to meet you." Glen shook Nadine's hand, then turned to Jesse. "Think I could talk to you for a second?"

"Uh, okay." Jesse didn't know what it was about, but Glen wouldn't have interrupted them if it wasn't important. He turned to Nadine. "Wait here. I'll be back."

Glen headed into the woods and Jesse walked alongside him.

"So what's up?" Jesse asked.

"Elvis saw you and Nadine this morning, down at the cove," Glen said.

"Oh yeah? Figures he'd spy on me."

Glen gave him a super-serious look. "Listen, I was a lot like you when I was your age. But Annie's worried. She wanted me to talk to you about it. She thinks that kind of behavior can be dangerous."

Jesse thought he understood. It was because Willy had been in the wild for two years.

"That's what Nadine thought too," he said. "But I know it's safe. I know exactly what I'm doing."

"I used to think that, too," Glen said.

"Hey, come on," Jesse said. "I'm practically an expert."

"I used to think *that* too," Glen said with a chuckle. He put his arm around Jesse's shoulder. "I know you're just going with your feelings. You're a good, smart kid. But it can lead to other things."

Other things? Jesse didn't have a clue what Glen meant. "Like what?"

"Well . . ." Glen paused and cleared his throat. "Like sex."

Jesse stopped and stared at him. Swimming with Willy could lead to sex? "Glen, are you feeling okay?"

"I'm fine," Glen said. "Why?"

"Because I don't know what you're talking about," Jesse said.

"I'm talking about you kissing Nadine," Glen said.

"I never kissed Nadine," Jesse said. "Who said I kissed Nadine?"

"I'll give you three guesses," Glen said.

Before Jesse could say anything, Glen turned

and headed back toward the campsite. Jesse had a definite feeling he was going to take care of Elvis. He headed back toward Nadine. She was still sitting on the rocks, looking out at the straits with the binoculars.

"What'd he want?" she asked.

"Nothing important," Jesse said. "Could I use those for a second?"

"Okay."

Jesse took the glasses and aimed them back through the trees at the campsite. He watched Glen stop in front of Elvis and say something. Then Elvis went into his tent. Glen zipped it closed. Jesse handed the binoculars back to Nadine and grinned. Looked as if Elvis had just gotten himself grounded.

"Was that your brother?" Nadine asked. "He doesn't look anything like you."

"We have different dads," Jesse said. He really didn't want to talk about that little pain, so he pointed back at the straits. "Any sign of Willy's pod?"

"Maybe they went back to the rubbing rocks," Nadine said.

"I wonder why they like it so much?" Jesse asked.

"Nobody really knows," Nadine said. "But it must feel good to them or they wouldn't do it."

"Jesse?" Glen called down through the trees. "Dinnertime."

Jesse turned back to Nadine. "Guess I gotta go. Want to go back to the rubbing rocks and check it out tomorrow?"

"Okay," Nadine said.

"Cool." Jesse started back toward the campsite. "See you then."

Jesse waved and turned toward the campsite. He couldn't wait for tomorrow.

10

The next morning, down at the cove, Jesse dove into the clear Pacific water. Nadine followed. They swam out to the swim platform. Below they could see the dark forms of Willy, Luna, and Littlespot rubbing themselves against the bottom. Jesse took a deep breath and dove down. Nadine was right behind him. They swam right into the group of whales and then rose with them to the surface.

Jesse's head popped out of the water. Then Nadine's. Then Luna's, Littlespot's, and Willy's.

Luna started to chatter happily at them.

"Willy's sister sure likes to blab," Nadine said with a laugh.

The whales dove again and the kids dove after them. They played like that for a while. Then Jesse noticed that Littlespot was gone. He and Nadine swam to the surface and treaded water. Jesse looked around.

"What's wrong?" Nadine asked.

"Littlespot. He's — " Jesse didn't finish the sentence. Over on the rocks, Elvis was shooting Littlespot with his water pistol. Littlespot was squirting water back with his mouth. Elvis laughed hysterically. Jesse felt a cloud forming.

"That little creep," he said. "He follows me everywhere."

"He looks up to you," Nadine said.

"No way."

"He does," Nadine insisted. "You want to ask him to join us?"

It was obvious that Elvis didn't know they were watching him. He ran along the rocks, laughing and shooting Littlespot with the water gun. Meanwhile, Littlespot spit water at Elvis.

"Let's leave him alone," Jesse said. "It's the first time I've ever seen him have fun."

Jesse and Nadine kept diving and swimming with Willy and Luna. At one point, Willy started to nudge Nadine with his snout. Nadine nervously grabbed Jesse's hand and held on tight. Jesse hoped she'd never let go.

The next time they came to the surface, another whale voice broke the stillness with a shrill whistle and chatter. Willy and his brother and sister spyhopped for a moment, then all headed out to sea.

"What was it?" Nadine asked.

"Catspaw," Jesse said. "I bet she wants to hunt."

"Too bad," Nadine said. "We were having fun."

He and Nadine swam toward a small crescent-shaped sandy beach beside the cove. Nadine had a funny look on her face.

"Uh, what's up?" Jesse asked uncomfortably.

"I was wrong about you," Nadine said. She started to move her face closer. She closed her eyes. The next thing Jesse knew, her lips touched his. He closed his eyes. Goose bumps ran up and down his arms. They were actually kissing. This was . . . amazing.

The day passed quickly. They swam together, and walked along the beach looking at rocks and shells and pieces of driftwood. They held hands and kissed. The whole day had a dreamy, magical quality. Jesse had never spent a day like it before.

Then too soon, it seemed, it had to end. Dinnertime was approaching and Jesse realized he was starving.

"I have to get back," Nadine said. "Randolph must be wondering where I am."

"Yeah, I guess I better get back too," Jesse said.

They climbed back up on the rocks and pulled their clothes on over their damp bathing suits. Nadine took a brush out of her pocket and brushed the sand out of her hair.

Jesse kissed her again. Every time his lips

touched hers, a magical shiver raced through him.

"See you tomorrow?" Nadine said after they pulled apart.

"Count on it," Jesse said with a wink.

They went their separate ways — Nadine back to the Orca Institute and Jesse back to the campground. Glen and Annie were just making dinner over the campfire when he arrived. They asked a couple of questions about how he'd spent his day, but when his answers were vague, they dropped it.

Later it grew dark and they went into their tents and got into their sleeping bags. Once again Jesse lay awake, thinking about Nadine, Willy, and finally, his mother. Meanwhile, Mr. "I Never Sleep" was out cold in the sleeping bag beside him. There was one thing that Jesse still couldn't understand. All those years when he'd been shuttled from one foster home to the next, and then finally had gone to live on the streets with Perry and the rest of those kids . . . all those years Elvis had been living with his mom.

There was a question Jesse had to ask. He hated waking Elvis up, but he knew he wouldn't sleep that night until he had the answer. He picked up a flashlight and shined it into Elvis's eyes.

"Elvis, are you asleep?" he asked.

"No," Elvis answered.

"I have to ask you something," Jesse said. "Did

CONSERVATION

EVINRUDE

WN 6250 NC

Mom ever talk about before you were born? Like about when she lived out here?"

Elvis was quiet. Jesse was glad he didn't just mouth off one of his wise-guy replies.

"No," Elvis said.

Jesse could feel the weight of disappointment start to settle down on his shoulders. "Did she ever talk about my dad?"

"No."

Jesse took a big breath and let it out slowly. "Did she . . . ever talk about me?"

Elvis was quiet again. Then he shook his head slowly. Jesse felt a pang deep in his heart and rolled onto his back and stared at the ceiling of the tent. He didn't want Elvis to see his face. How could she not have talked about him? He was her kid!

"She had problems," Elvis said, as if he knew what Jesse was thinking.

"Like what?" Jesse asked.

"She lied all the time," Elvis said. "She said she loved me."

He sounded like he didn't believe it.

"Maybe she did," Jesse said.

"She said she'd never leave," Elvis said.

Jesse heard the hurt in his voice. He knew exactly how Elvis felt. He hated to admit it, but he and his little half brother had a lot in common.

11

That night Jesse dreamed that he heard the faint cry of orcas coming through a deep fog. They were calling for help. He tried to find them, but he couldn't see through the fog. They just kept calling and calling. . . .

He opened his eyes. It was early. The light filtered through the tent, and the air was damp and cold. There, he heard it again, so faint it might have been a bird or even his imagination. But Jesse didn't think so. An orca was out there somewhere, crying for help.

He pulled on his clothes and slipped out of the tent. The air was chilly and he reached back in and grabbed a jacket. He pulled it on and then stood perfectly still.

There it was again. Orcas calling. They sounded scared. Jesse headed down through the woods toward the water. He wondered what could have happened. Had one of them been hit by a boat in the night? Or gotten caught in a fisherman's gill net? He stopped to listen again.

He heard the orcas cry. Then *crackle . . . snap!* A different sound. Made by someone coming through the woods behind him. Jesse spun around. Elvis was working his way down the path, in and around the trees, pushing branches out of his way. Jesse felt a moment of annoyance, but it quickly passed.

"Come on," he whispered.

Elvis looked up, surprised to see him. Then he nodded and followed Jesse down the trail. Now he could hear the calls more clearly. They were wails, filled with despair. Jesse quickened his pace.

"Hear that?" he said.

"What is it?" Elvis asked, following behind.

"Orcas."

"They sound sad."

"Yeah." Jesse scurried down toward the cove. By now the red sun had peaked up over the mountains across the straits. The rippling water sparkled red. Jesse suddenly skidded to a stop on the dirt path.

"Elvis, look!" He pointed down through the trees to the cove. Littlespot was spyhopping in the middle of the cove, calling out plaintively toward the beach as if something were there. But the rocks were blocking Jesse's view.

Jesse hurried down the path and stopped on the rocks. Now he could see the beach. A whale was lying halfway out of the water. She had a white crescent-shaped patch on her dorsal fin. Small waves were splashing against her sides.

"It's Luna, Willy's sister," he yelled back to Elvis. "She's beached!"

Jesse scrambled over the rocks down to Luna. Out in the water, Littlespot came as close as he could, calling out to her unhappily. As Jesse got closer to Luna, he slowed down. Something was wrong. She was bobbing listlessly in the shallow water. Jesse walked into the water and rubbed her head. A slick oily goo came off on his hands. Jesse stared at them.

"What is it?" Elvis said.

"I think it's oil," Jesse said. He looked back down at Luna. The oil was all over her head. It was even covering her eyes. Whitish mucous was slowly draining out of her blowhole.

"There must've been an oil spill," Jesse said. "This is bad. She's really sick."

"Why's she facing the beach?" Elvis asked.

"They get confused when they're sick," Jesse said.

"What should we do?" Elvis asked.

"You gotta go wake Glen," Jesse said. "Get him down here as fast as you can. No, wait, have him call Randolph first! We'll all try to get Luna back in the water."

Elvis started to back away. "What are you gonna do?"

Jesse rubbed Luna's head. "I'm gonna stay here with her until help comes."

Elvis turned and started to run back up the beach. Standing knee deep in the cove, Jesse patted Luna on the head.

"You're gonna be okay," he said softly.

But Luna's eyes were dull and the most she could muster was a low, helpless whine.

"Yeah." Jesse stroked her sides softly. "Don't feel like talking. I understand."

Ker-splash! A sudden splash caught Jesse by surprise. It was Willy, using his tail to splash water on his sister. Near him Littlespot also tried to splash water on his sister, but his splashes weren't nearly as effective. Jesse had to back away so that he didn't get soaked. Somehow Willy knew that he had to keep Luna wet. Today the sun would be their enemy. Luna's black skin would absorb the heat and light of the sun, but if it dried, Luna would die a slow painful death.

Finally Glen, Annie, and Elvis came running down to the beach. At the same time Randolph and Nadine arrived in the truck.

"Jesse," Glen said, "what's this whale doing halfway out of the water?"

"It's Luna, Willy's sister," Jesse said desperately. "She's sick. I think she's dying."

Randolph joined them and nodded grimly.

"What's going on, Randolph?" Glen asked.

"Radio says an oil tanker ran aground on Lawson Reef last night," he said. "The darn thing's leaking crude oil everywhere. It's a major spill. This stuff is poison to everything that lives in the water. It could devastate every form of wildlife around here for miles."

"What can we do?" Annie asked.

"First thing is try to help Luna," Randolph said. He went back to the truck and took some white gauze and a plastic bag out of a first aid kit. Then he headed down toward the beached whale. They all watched as he laid the gauze over her blowhole, collecting some of the whitish mucous. Then he dropped the gauze into the plastic bag and sealed it.

"Nadine!" He waved to her.

"Yes?" Nadine came down toward them. Randolph handed her the bag.

"Run this back to the institute," he said. "Tell them it's from me, and it's an emergency. They've probably all heard about the spill by now. They'll know what's going on."

"They gonna analyze it?" Elvis asked.

"Yes," Randolph said. "In the meantime, the rest of us are going to try to get Luna back into the water. Let's go."

Everyone except Elvis, who was too small to help, waded into the inlet and started to work to get Luna off the rocks and back into the water.

As soon as Willy saw what they were doing, he stopped splashing his sister and waited.

"Okay, now we don't want to hurt her," Randolph said. "Glen and Annie, you each take one of her flukes. Jesse and I will take the tail. Each time a wave comes in we'll try to slide her out on the runoff."

Luna was nearly as big as Willy. But working together, they managed to slide the whale back into the water. But Luna just bobbed in the shallows. Her breathing was still labored and her eyes were still glassy. Randolph and Jesse stood waist-deep in the water.

"I'm not sure getting her into the water has helped much," Glen said. "She still looks pretty sick."

"She needs something, Randolph," Jesse said.

"As soon as we heard about the oil spill we called in Kate Haley," Randolph said. "She's our vet from the mainland."

Now that Luna was floating in the small inlet, Willy began to swim in circles around her. Littlespot followed his older brother. Standing in the water, Jesse realized that his friend was swimming right toward him.

As Willy came closer, Jesse reached out to pet him proudly. "Way to go, Willy. You helped save your sis — "

Jesse thought Willy would stop and let him pet him, but the big orca swam right past, ignoring him. Surprised, Jesse turned to Randolph.

"What's the matter with him?"

"His sister is dying," Randolph replied grimly.

Out in the inlet, Willy circled Luna, as if he were standing guard.

"But we're all on the same side, aren't we?" Jesse asked in a concerned voice.

"It's hard to tell what he's thinking right now," Randolph replied.

12

The news that three orcas were in the cove began to spread. The coast guard arrived and set up an emergency rescue station for all the creatures that would be affected by the spill. They put up a tent and started a communications center to organize the rescue effort. Tourists and local newspaper reporters began to show up. Soon the police arrived and used yellow tape to keep people back. Meanwhile, down on the beach, Jesse and the others listened to the news on the truck's radio.

"The Dakar, *a forty-year-old Liberian oil tanker, ran aground on Lawson Reef last night, spilling thousands of gallons of raw crude oil into the water."*

"If it's forty years old you know it was a single-hulled piece of rusty tin," said Nadine, who'd come back from the lab.

"Wait a minute," Annie said. "I did a story on oil tankers once. I thought after 1990 they all had to have double hulls to prevent this kind of accident."

"All the tankers *built* after 1990 had to have them," Randolph explained. "If they were built before 1990 they were exempt from the ruling. A few companies had their older ships retrofitted with a double inner lining, but it was strictly voluntary."

"So, in a perverse way, by requiring double hulls after 1990 that made the older single-hulled ships more valuable to the oil companies," Annie guessed.

"Look, a plane." Elvis pointed in the air and they saw a small bush plane with double pontoons gliding into the cove for a landing.

"That'll be Kate," Randolph said.

The plane landed and taxied to the dock where the *Little Dipper* was tied up. It was on the other side of the cove, where the emergency rescue effort was being set up. Jesse and the others watched as a woman wearing jeans and a red jacket climbed out of the plane and was greeted by a man in a blue coast guard uniform. The woman had shoulder-length brown hair and short bangs. Together they walked down the dock toward the tented headquarters of the rescue effort.

"Come on, Jesse," Randolph said. "We better go talk to her."

Jesse nodded.

Dozens of people were rushing around, studying

maps, and talking on portable telephones. A lot of the activity was centered around a large map of the straits and islands.

"Kate," Randolph said.

She turned around. As soon as she saw Randolph, she smiled. "Randolph!"

"I'm glad you're here," Randolph said, handing her a clipboard he'd been carrying.

"So what've we got?" Dr. Haley asked, looking down at the clipboard.

"Immature female got into the crude oil. Looks like a pretty severe respiratory infection."

"How long ago was the culture taken?" Dr. Haley asked.

"Three hours."

Dr. Haley looked somber. "I heard her struggling to breathe after I got off the plane. We better get to her now, before she gets any worse."

"This is Jesse," Randolph said, putting his hand on Jesse's shoulder. "He's the one who found them."

In the midst of the whirlwind of activity around them, Dr. Haley focused on Jesse as if there were no one else on the dock. "So, I finally get to meet you," she said with a smile. "Randolph's told me all about you."

Jesse was surprised to hear that.

"If these whales recover," Dr. Haley said, "finding them when you did will certainly be the thing that saved their lives."

"*If* they recover?" Jesse repeated nervously. "Is there a chance they won't?"

"I'm going to do my best, Jesse," Dr. Haley said.

Jesse had heard that tone of voice a million times in his life. It was the tone adults used when they couldn't make a promise. It meant, *Maybe . . .*

"The *Zodiac*'s ready, Kate," someone yelled from the entrance to the tent.

"Be right there," Dr. Haley said. She turned back to Jesse. She must have seen the worried look on his face because she gave him a reassuring smile. "Hey, don't worry. I'm really good at this."

Dr. Haley turned and headed toward the dock. Jesse gave Randolph a worried look.

"You remember what happened at the adventure park," Jesse reminded him. "Willy doesn't like doctors."

"She's one of the best," Randolph said.

"*You* know that," Jesse said. "But Willy doesn't."

"Come on," Randolph said, heading back out of the tent. "Let's go watch."

They climbed up on the rocks overlooking the cove. Nadine was already there, looking through the binoculars. But she wasn't looking at the whales, instead she was looking out to sea.

"What is it?" Randolph asked.

Instead of answering, Nadine handed him the

binoculars. Randolph looked through them, then lowered the glasses. He looked pale.

"What?" Jesse asked.

"The oil slick is moving this way," Randolph said. "If Luna doesn't get better fast, she'll be trapped in the cove."

"Willy will never leave his sister," Nadine said. "And Littlespot does everything Willy does."

At that instant, Jesse realized what she meant. The three whales would stay in the cove. And it would be covered with oil.

"Then Catspaw will lose her family," he said. He wanted to hold Nadine's hand, but he couldn't with everyone there.

"How's it going?" someone asked.

They turned and found Glen and Annie climbing up on the rocks toward them.

"Don't know yet," Randolph said.

Out in the cove, Dr. Haley and a few others were in the inflatable *Zodiac*, moving toward Luna. Jesse raised his binoculars.

"Oh, no!" he gasped.

"What's wrong?" Annie asked.

"They're going to inject Luna with a needle bigger than my arm," Jesse said.

"It's got to be that long to get through the layers of blubber," Randolph said.

"Try explaining that to Willy," Jesse said doubtfully.

Not far from Luna, Willy spyhopped, watching

the boat approach. As the *Zodiac* got close to Luna, it slowed down. The long, silvery hypodermic needle glinted in the sun.

Suddenly, Willy submerged.

"See, he's getting out of the way," Annie said.

Jesse had his doubts. A second later, the *Zodiac* rose slightly as if something had lifted it from underneath. In the boat, Dr. Haley and the others shouted with surprise and held onto the sides. The *Zodiac* began to move away from Luna.

"Why are they leaving?" Elvis asked.

"Willy's pushing them," Jesse said, watching through the binoculars. The boat was moving faster and faster. The people on board were struggling to keep their balance.

"He's trying to protect his sister," Nadine said.

"Yeah, but that means Luna won't get the medicine she needs," said Elvis.

"You can't expect Willy to understand that," Randolph said. "Especially since he's been in the wild for the last two years."

"But he remembered me," Jesse said.

"Yes." Randolph nodded gravely. "He remembered *you*. But in every other way this is a whole new ball game."

13

Now that everyone knew Jesse and Randolph were the friends of Dr. Haley, they were allowed to come and go from the command center as they pleased. Jesse and Nadine got to listen in on the TV interviews as the commander of the Coastal Marine Patrol explained to reporters how they were putting a boom on the water around the *Dakar* to try to prevent any more oil from escaping. Since oil was lighter than water, it always floated on the surface. A boom was a long tube filled with air that was laid out around the oil and stopped it from drifting everywhere. He added that despite their best efforts the winds and ocean currents could still mess up everything.

A little while later a black limousine arrived at the tent and several men got out. They all seemed to focus on one man in a black suit. He had dark hair and an athletic build. He wore wire-rimmed glasses and carried a black briefcase.

"Who is he?" Jesse whispered into Randolph's ear.

"His name's Milner and he's from the oil company," Randolph whispered back.

"What's he doing here?" Nadine asked, bristling.

"He says he wants to help. He's going to meet with Kate in a second."

Jesse felt himself grow tense. "That's bull. If he wanted to help, how come he let his company use that crummy old oil tanker?"

"Because his company was gambling that a tragedy like this wouldn't happen," Randolph replied.

"They were gambling with the lives of millions of sea creatures," Nadine said angrily. "Including Willy and his brother and sister."

Randolph put his hand on Jesse's shoulder. "Now calm down. Everybody makes mistakes. Not that I'm any fan of oil companies, but let's at least give the man a chance and hear what he has to say."

Meanwhile, Milner and Dr. Haley had started to talk. Randolph, Jesse, and Nadine moved closer and listened to what they were saying.

"Wait a minute, Dr. Haley," Milner said. "I asked you what it would take to save these whales. You gave me a shopping list and I provided everything you asked for. I paid for this camp, I got you the boats and equipment, didn't I?"

Dr. Haley nodded. "Yes, you wrote a check."

"And now you're telling me you can't help that whale because her older brother beat you up?" Milner asked.

"These orcas are very agitated," Dr. Haley tried to explain. "They don't trust people. You can understand that, can't you? I mean, given the circumstances."

"I just want to save these poor whales and avert a tragedy," Milner said.

Jesse was surprised that the man sounded so sincere, but Dr. Haley quickly pointed out why.

"I think you want to avert a public relations nightmare," she corrected him.

But Milner didn't get angry or defensive. "Listen, doctor, by definition an oil company is a public relations nightmare. Everyone wants their oil, and they want it cheap, but nobody wants to clean up the mess afterwards. That's just part of the business. The reason I'm here is that I can't sit by and watch innocent lives lost when we could be doing something about it."

Jesse was surprised when Randolph stepped forward. "That's an impressive speech. I wonder if you mean it."

Milner took off his glasses and cleaned them with a handkerchief. He squinted at Randolph. "What if I do?"

Randolph glanced out of the corner of his eye at Jesse. "Then I think I can solve your problem."

Solving the problem of the whales meant talking to Glen and Annie. A little while later, Jesse, Randolph, Dr. Haley, and Milner showed up at the campsite. Both Annie and Glen looked surprised.

Milner held out his hand. "I'm John Milner from Benbrook Oil and I need to talk to you about Jesse."

Glen shook his hand and then they all sat down and discussed the plan Randolph had suggested.

"I'm not going to lie to you, Jesse," Milner said. "This is an awful situation, and my company is to blame for it. It's very important to me that no harm comes to these whales. And that, according to Randolph, is where you come in."

"I don't like it," Annie said, shaking her head. "We're talking about killer whales. I won't allow you to put Jesse in danger."

"But it's Willy," Jesse said.

"He's been living in the wild for two years," Annie reminded him. "No one knows what that means."

"Jesse's just a kid," Glen told the others.

"I won't allow him to be put in danger either," Dr. Haley said. "I assure you it will be all right. But we need him."

"I could help out," Elvis said. "Littlespot likes me. I could — "

Glen raised a finger to his lips and quieted Jesse's half brother. Elvis narrowed his eyes and looked ticked off.

"The point is, Willy trusts Jesse," Milner said.

"And he doesn't trust you," Jesse replied.

"Willy thinks he's protecting Luna," Dr. Haley explained. "But by keeping us away from her he's really killing her. Jesse is his only friend. Jesse can help Willy and save Luna."

"You promise no harm will come to Jesse?" Annie asked.

"I promise," Dr. Haley said.

Glen and Annie looked at each other. Jesse could see that they'd reached an agreement.

"Okay, Mr. Milner," Annie said.

"Great." Milner slapped his hands together and smiled.

"Wait a minute," Jesse said. Everyone turned and looked at him. "They agreed, but I'm not sure I have."

"What do you mean?" Milner looked puzzled.

"I'll convince Willy to let you help Luna," Jesse said, "but you have to promise to get Willy, Luna, and Littlespot back to their mother."

Milner was quiet for a moment. Then he said, "I can't promise that. I'm not God, Jesse. I don't know if the whales will get better. And there are a lot of people to answer to here."

"But it's your oil that's killing Luna," Jesse said. "If Luna dies, everybody's gonna see it on the six o'clock news, and everybody's gonna blame you."

Milner raised his hands in a helpless gesture. "I'm doing everything I can."

"Just promise me you'll at least *try* to get them back to their mother," Jesse said.

Milner nodded. "All right. I promise."

Just then, Elvis got up and marched off into the woods. Annie got up and followed him. For a moment Jesse wondered if something was wrong. Then he looked back at Milner.

"Okay," he said. "Now there's just one thing I'm gonna need."

"You name it," Milner said.

Despite the dire circumstances, Jesse couldn't help smiling. "Chocolate," he said.

14

Jesse didn't know what was going on with Elvis and Annie, and he didn't have time to find out either. Every wasted second was a step closer to death for Luna. They all hurried back down to the emergency command post.

A little while later Jesse stood on the dock, looking out into the cove at Willy. His friend was still circling Luna. Littlespot followed him. On the other side of the dock, Dr. Haley and some other crewmen were preparing to go out in the *Zodiac* again.

Jesse loaded a plastic garbage bag and some other supplies into a small yellow rubber raft beside the dock. Then he got in and began to row. By now there were people watching from all over the place. They were on the pier, up on the rocks, even in boats outside the cove.

Jesse rowed out to the swim platform. Dr. Haley and her crew stayed on their boat on the dock, careful not to attract Willy's attention. Jesse tied the raft to the swim platform and climbed up. Sitting on the edge of the platform with his feet in the water, he started to play the harmonica.

Willy didn't respond. He just kept circling Luna. Jesse played louder. Willy *still* didn't react.

Jesse lowered the harmonica from his lips. Could it be that Willy was ignoring him? That he just didn't care?

Jesse brought the harmonica back to his lips and played again. Willy kept circling Luna. Jesse played louder. Willy veered slightly from his course, as if he couldn't decide which way to go. Jesse realized it must have been hard for him to leave his sick sister. But he gradually turned away and swam toward Jesse, as if hoping the boy might have some answer to the terrible fate his sister faced.

"That-a-boy, Willy," Jesse said. "It's me, your friend."

He knew he'd caught Willy's eye. The big whale swam toward the platform.

Wait a minute! Suddenly Jesse realized that Willy wasn't stopping.

Thunk! Willy hit the platform with his snout. The platform rocked in the water. It seemed like he was trying to push it away, just as he'd pushed away the *Zodiac* that morning.

"Willy, it's me, Jesse," Jesse yelled.

But Willy just backed up and swam ahead again.

Thunk! He rammed the platform again. Jesse

lost his balance and had to hold on to keep from getting knocked off.

Bonk! Something else hit the platform, but barely shook it. Jesse looked down into the water and saw Littlespot, imitating his big brother.

Willy backed up again and prepared to charge the swim platform again.

"Stop it, Willy. I'm not going to hurt you," Jesse said. "I want to help."

But Willy just glared at him and emitted a low pitched whistle that sounded to Jesse like a growl.

"Willy . . . ?" Jesse couldn't believe his friend would turn on him like that.

The growl was followed by a groan. But it didn't come from Willy, it came from Luna. Both Jesse and Willy looked at the sick whale, floating haplessly in the cove. Then Willy turned back to Jesse. Jesse reached into his trash bag and pulled out a large salmon. He held it over the water and gave Willy the signal to open his mouth.

"How about some chocolate, huh?" Jesse said. "For old time's sake?"

Willy eyed the "chocolate" but didn't move.

"I know you probably eat live ones now," Jesse said in a soft voice. "But this is the best I could do. So what do you say? All I want to do is help Luna and get you all back to your mom."

Willy moved a little closer, then stopped as if he still couldn't make up his mind.

"Please, Willy?" Jesse said, barely above a whisper.

Willy moved a little closer and opened his mouth. Jesse looked into it and once again saw those teeth, only they looked bigger.

Willy came closer. Jesse realized the whale could have swallowed him whole if it wanted to. He held his breath and shut his eyes. He didn't know what Willy was going to do. He thought the killer whale was his friend, but you couldn't know for sure. Not after two years in the wild. Not after watching Luna get so sick. Jesse felt something touch the salmon. Opening his eyes, he saw Willy touching it with his big pink tongue. Jesse laid the fish down on Willy's tongue. Willy swallowed it and chattered. He seemed happy.

A distant cheer came from the crowd watching.

A wave of relief swept through Jesse. He leaned forward and patted his friend on the head. "Hey, that's the old Willy. I promise you I'm not gonna let you down, pal."

Willy stayed by the swimming platform and let Jesse rub him on the head. With his free hand, Jesse waved at Dr. Haley.

"It's okay," he yelled.

On the fishing boat, Dr. Haley give him the thumbs-up sign. She gave her crew an order and the boat began to move slowly out into the cove toward Luna.

Almost immediately, Jesse felt a shiver run

through Willy. Jesse kept stroking him and talking softly.

"That's Dr. Haley," he said. "She's going to help Luna."

Jesse watched the boat pull up alongside Luna. He could feel Willy's anxiety.

Dr. Haley leaned over the side of the *Zodiac* and stroked Luna's head. "It's going to be okay, Luna."

But Jesse could hear how the whale was struggling for each breath.

"You don't sound so good," Dr. Haley said softly. Then she turned to Jesse. "We have to get her to raise her fluke."

Jesse understood why she'd told him that. He turned to Willy in the water. "You have to show Luna what to do, Willy. If you do it, she'll do it."

Jesse gave Willy the sign to raise his fluke. But Willy didn't move. Jesse didn't think it was because Willy didn't want to move. It was just that Willy was probably too upset to want to perform tricks.

Jesse gave him the sign again. "Come on, Willy. For your sister's sake."

As if Willy had heard him, he raised his right fluke. Nearby, Luna watched. Then slowly, painstakingly, she raised her fluke.

"Way to go, boy." Jesse stroked Willy on the head.

"That's good, Luna," Dr. Haley said softly. "That's really good."

Jesse watched as Dr. Haley gave Luna her shot. Once again Jesse turned to Willy and patted him on the head.

"Nice going, Willy," he said. "You just saved your sister's life."

15

They left Willy and Luna alone after that. Jesse got the raft and rowed it back to the dock. Dr. Haley followed in the *Zodiac*. Nadine waited on the dock.

"That was really brave," she said.

Jesse nodded. "I . . . I had to do it."

"I know."

Their eyes locked. Jesse felt the same emotions he'd felt that day they'd kissed on the beach. He felt drawn to her as if by magnetism, but they were surrounded by people. He was too shy to do anything.

The *Zodiac* docked and Dr. Haley climbed out. "We better go see what's going on," she said, heading toward the communications tent. Jesse and Nadine walked with her. Inside the tent, John Milner, the man from the oil company, was on the phone. When he saw Jesse and Dr. Haley, he quickly hung up and smiled. Jesse couldn't be sure, but it seemed as if the man were acting a little guilty about something.

"You hit it out of the park, kid," he said. "I'm impressed."

There was something about the guy that sent out warning signals to Jesse, but he couldn't quite figure out what it was. Randolph joined them and patted Jesse on the shoulder.

"Nice going, Jesse. I'm proud of you," he said.

"It was the only way to save Luna's life," Jesse said.

"All we can do now is wait and see how she responds," Dr. Haley said. "You did good work, Jesse. It took a lot of guts."

"I was scared to death." The words blurted out of his mouth before he could stop them.

Dr. Haley smiled. "Well, I've got news for you. When you've been doing this as long as I have, you'll be twice as scared."

One of Dr. Haley's assistants came up and took Dr. Haley and Randolph aside. He pointed at the map of the straits and spoke in somber tones. When he was finished, Randolph and Dr. Haley turned back to Jesse and Nadine. They both looked considerably less pleased than they had before.

"What's wrong?" Jesse asked.

"The oil slick," Randolph said, pointing back at the map. "The currents are pushing it right toward the cove. We don't have a lot of time."

Jesse looked at Dr. Haley. "Can't we do anything?"

"Not yet," she said. "First we have to see how Luna reacts to the antibiotics."

There was nothing they could do but wait. The day passed slowly. Much of the relief efforts turned toward the other animals affected by the oil spill. Hundreds of birds, otters, and seals, soaked with black oil and too weak to fight, were brought in to be cleaned and saved. But Jesse heard that for every creature that was saved, a dozen more would die before help could reach them.

As day turned to dusk and the sun slanted through the trees to the west, Jesse stood at the edge of the dock with Nadine. Willy was no longer circling Luna. As if sensing that something were being done to help his little sister, he now floated nearby watching and waiting. Luna bobbed quietly in the center of the cove, as if all her strength and energy were being devoted toward becoming well again.

On the dock, Nadine stood with her arms wrapped around her. She was staring way out at the waters of the straits. Jesse gave her a curious look. He wondered what she was thinking, but didn't want to ask.

"Their mom is probably going crazy from worrying," Nadine said, somehow knowing Jesse was wondering.

"Catspaw?"

Nadine nodded.

"I wish I could tell her not to worry," Jesse said. "Luna's going to get better. I know she will. It's all going to be okay."

To his surprise, Nadine grimaced and quickly looked away as if he'd said something wrong.

"What is it?" Jesse asked.

Nadine turned back and glared angrily at him. "It's not *all* going to be okay, Jesse."

Jesse was surprised to see tears start to run out of her eyes.

"You have to think positive," Jesse said. "Luna's young. She's strong. She can beat it."

"I'm not talking about Luna," Nadine said. She waved her arm out at the water and islands. "I'm talking about all of this. It's all *ruined.* This is just your summer vacation. You can go home. But this is my backyard."

She was right. He would go home, but she had to stay in a world that had been scarred and would take years to recover. Nadine sniffed and tried to rub the tears out of her eyes. Jesse wished he had something to give her to help dab up the tears. But he didn't have a handkerchief or any tissues. Then he had an idea and reached for the pocket of his shirt.

Rippppppp! He tore it off his shirt and handed it to Nadine.

"Here," he said.

Nadine scowled through her tears at him. "What?"

"I don't have a Kleenex," Jesse explained. "This is the best I can do."

A small appreciative smile curled onto Nadine's lips. She took the pocket and blew her nose into it. Then she held it out toward him.

"Want your pocket back?"

"Naw, that's okay," Jesse said with a grin. "You can keep it."

The smile faded from Nadine's face. Fresh tears started to gather in the corners of her eyes. Very gently, Jesse reached over and wiped the tears away with his fingertips. Then he slid a little closer and put his arm around her shoulders. Together they stared out at the beautiful sights. The sun was setting, giving the distant islands a slightly golden glow. The water was blue and calm. It was a sight that had taken Mother Nature millions of years to create. But it would take man and his oil tankers only a few days to destroy.

It was dark when Jesse got back to the campsite. From the light glowing inside his tent, he knew that Elvis was already in his sleeping bag. Jesse pulled back the flap and was in for a shock. Elvis was lying in his sleeping bag, holding up the carved wooden orca Randolph had given to Jesse. It looked as if he were studying it.

"Who said you could touch that?" Jesse asked

as he ducked down and went into the tent.

"The President of the United States," Elvis replied. "He announced it on TV. Where were you?"

Jesse was used to Elvis by now. There was no sense in getting mad. Besides, the kid hadn't hurt it or anything. Jesse pulled off his shoes and pants. "I didn't know there were any TVs in this campground."

"Oh, yeah," Elvis replied without missing a beat. "Guy across the way's got a twenty-seven inch Trinitron."

Jesse slid into his sleeping bag. One thing you could say about Elvis, he had a fertile imagination. Meanwhile, the kid was looking at the carving again.

"It's pretty cool, huh?" Jesse said.

"Yeah. What's it for anyway?"

Jesse was surprised. Elvis didn't often ask questions. Most of the time he was too busy pretending he already knew the answers. Jesse rolled over and looked at the kid in the warm glow of the kerosene lantern.

"You really want to know?" he asked.

"Not if it's a long story," Elvis replied.

"Well, it's not too long," Jesse said, playing along.

"Oh, okay."

"There was a young Haida Indian named Natselane," Jesse said. "He lived a long time ago, like before there were whales."

"But there's *always* been whales," Elvis said.

"Chill a little, okay?" Jesse said. "This is a legend. So one day Natselane got lost and couldn't find his way home. And he carved the first ever whale out of a log."

Elvis made a face like he didn't believe it. "Come off it. A big wooden fish?"

"You want to hear this story or not?" Jesse asked.

"I bet the big wooden fish comes to life and it's a whale, right?" Elvis guessed.

"That's right," said Jesse.

"And I bet Natselane gets back to his family too," Elvis added.

The words hung between them in the lantern light. *Back to his family* . . . It was something that would never happen for Jesse and Elvis.

"Yeah," Jesse said softly. "That's what happened. Natselane prayed so hard to get back to his family that the whale came to life. And Natselane rode on the back of the whale all the way home."

Jesse waited for a wisecrack from Elvis, but this time none came. The kid was thinking about it. He was probably thinking about that word, too. . . . Home.

16

Someone was shaking his shoulder. Jesse opened his eyes. It was morning. Sunlight was filtering through the gauzy tent material. Jesse turned his head and found Elvis looking down at him.

"Why are you on my side of the tent?" Jesse asked, feeling a little irritable about being awakened.

"Oh." Elvis backed up to his side of the tent.

Jesse studied him. "You're already dressed?"

"Yeah," Elvis said eagerly. "Let's go down to the cove and check on the fish."

The fish . . . orcas . . . Willy and his brother and sister. Jesse sat up and started to pull his clothes on.

"They're not fish," he said. "They're mammals."

"What's a mammal?" Elvis asked.

"I'll tell you when you're older." Jesse pulled on his shoes. He didn't want to take time just then to explain it all. A few moments later he pushed back the tent flaps and crawled out. Elvis followed. Glen and Annie were already up.

They all started down the trail toward the cove.

Jesse saw Randolph and Nadine coming up the path toward them.

"I was just coming to get you," Randolph said. He looked grim and in a hurry.

"What is it?" Jesse asked.

"We've got a problem," Randolph said.

Before Jesse could ask more, Randolph turned and hurried back down the trail. Jesse and the others followed. As they reached the cove, Jesse saw a group of people huddled around something at the shore. Some of the people were on the beach and some were knee deep in the water.

It wasn't until he got closer that he saw why they were there. It was Luna! She was half-beached again. The people crowding around her were trying to get her back into the water. Jesse started down the beach toward her.

"No, Jesse." Randolph grabbed his arm. "Nadine will stay here with Luna. You're coming with me."

"Where?" Jesse asked.

Randolph pointed at his pickup truck, parked along the road.

"Luna's not any better," Randolph said. "We have to try something different."

"Like what?" Jesse asked.

"I'll explain as we go," Randolph said.

“I’m coming too,” Elvis said, following them.

“Stay here, Elvis,” Randolph said.

Jesse’s half brother stopped. “But I can help.”

The only thing Jesse could think about was Luna and how to help her. He wasn’t thinking about what Elvis needed.

“Not now,” he said quickly. “This is between me and Randolph.”

Randolph and Jesse jumped into the pickup. Randolph shoved it into gear and they started off down the road.

“Okay, now what’s the plan?” Jesse asked.

Randolph glanced at him out of the corner of his eye. “There are other medicines besides the one Dr. Haley believes in.”

“Indian medicine?” Jesse guessed.

Randolph nodded. Now he knew why Randolph had waited until they were alone. There were plenty of people who would have laughed at Randolph, but he wasn’t one of them. Besides, nothing Dr. Haley could do would help now. Randolph’s medicine might be Luna’s last chance.

A little while later, Randolph pulled the truck into one of those scenic view spots along the road. He pointed out the window at the straits.

“One of my spotters said Willy’s pod was around the point, just past the Noble Straits,” he said. He grabbed a pair of long black binoculars and climbed out of the truck. Jesse joined him as he stood at the side of the road and scanned the blue waters.

"There she is," Randolph said, pointing.

Jesse squinted. "I don't see anything."

"Here," Randolph handed him the binoculars.

Jesse pressed them to his eyes. All he saw were waves. Wait! Something black and white stuck out of the water. Jesse focused the binoculars on it. It was an orca.

"Who?" Jesse asked.

"Catspaw," Randolph said. "She's looking for her family. She'll look forever, or until she dies of a broken heart."

Jesse cupped his hands around his mouth. "Don't give up!" he shouted. "We'll get them back to you! I promise! You'll be a family again! It's going to be okay!"

He felt a hand settle onto his shoulder. It was Randolph.

"I know you want to help her," the older man said gently. "But we have to go."

They got back into the truck and drove farther. Soon the road turned off the coast and into the woods. Randolph pulled off to the side and stopped.

"What's here?" Jesse asked.

"Hopefully, what we need," Randolph said, pushing open the door. He got out and pulled an old wooden basket out of the back of the truck.

With Jesse following, he started into the woods, stopping here and there to pick a flower or a plant or a piece of bark off a tree. Then he stopped and started to dig around a plant with a flat wooden stick.

"Now what?" Jesse asked.

"This is skookum," Randolph explained. "We need the root."

"Why use a stick?" Jesse asked. "Why not a shovel."

"A flattened stick of alder is what my forefathers used," Randolph said as he dug. "Calling upon ancient spirits to heal sickness is a gift passed down from generation to generation. My grandmother taught me. Now I teach you."

Once the ground had been broken, Randolph reached down and carefully pulled up a tangle of bulbous roots. He carefully brushed the dirt off them and held them up for Jesse to see. Then he placed them in the basket and moved on. Soon he stopped at a tree and peeled back a piece of brown bark. Jesse was surprised to see that a light green fungus was growing underneath it.

Randolph took out a leather satchel. Then he used the alder stick to carefully scrape the fungus off the bark and into the bag.

"The plants and animals are our brothers in the world," Randolph said. "We are of the same family. Knowing this is part of what it means to have medicine roots."

They walked downhill and came to a small spring of clear water burbling out of the ground. There they squatted down and started to wash the roots and plants in the cold water below a waterfall.

"Now what?" Jesse asked.

"We make medicine," Randolph said, getting up.

They rode in the truck back toward the Orca Institute. They were just about to turn into the driveway when they saw Glen and Annie. Annie was jogging toward them, waving and shouting. Glen was following slowly behind her with a fed up look on his face.

"Hey, guys, wait up," Annie called.

Randolph stopped the truck and rolled down the window. "What up?"

"Have you seen Elvis?" Annie asked.

"No," said Jesse. "Why?"

"He's gone," said Glen. "And he took my wallet."

17

Annie explained what she thought had happened. They'd all been so concerned with Luna that morning that they'd been short with Elvis and had ignored his offers to help.

"He said he wanted to help and I told him not now," Glen said.

"And I told him to stand back and stay out of the way," Annie said. "I broke a promise."

"What promise?" Jesse asked.

"I promised he could help," Annie said. "I even did a spit-shake on it."

"That's serious," Glen said.

Jesse knew that was partly Glen's sarcastic sense of humor, but it was also partly true. To a kid Elvis's age, a spit-shake was an important thing.

"Should we help try to find him?" Jesse asked.

"Don't bother," Glen said.

Annie gave him a stern look. Glen rolled his eyes.

"Don't you ever get tired of this stuff?" he asked.

"His feelings are hurt," Annie said. "He needs us. He just needs someone to give him a break."

Glen shook his head. "Why do *we* have to do it? Why do we have to rehabilitate every troubled kid who comes within a mile of us?"

Jesse raised his hand.

"What?" Glen snapped.

"From what Annie told me, you weren't exactly an angel when you were a kid," Jesse said.

"Who asked you?" Glen said.

Annie smiled at him.

"Okay," Glen admitted. "I was trouble. I guess this is my punishment."

Annie wrapped her arms around Glen. "Tell me you didn't need someone to love you."

"That's why I have you," Glen said.

"And what about Elvis?" Annie asked. "Who does he have?"

Glen sighed. "You and me and Jesse."

"Leave me out of it," Jesse said.

"Jesse." Randolph gave him a stern look.

"Hey, only kidding," Jesse said. "You want us to help you find him?"

"No, you better keep trying to help Luna," Glen said. "We'll look for Elvis. We're on an island so he couldn't have gone too far. We just wanted you to be aware in case you see him."

"We'll keep our eyes open," Randolph said, taking the satchel out of the back of the pickup. Then he turned to Jesse. "Now come on, we don't have much time."

"Catch you later." Jesse waved to Glen and Annie and then followed Randolph into the institute.

Inside, in a modern science lab filled with modern equipment, Randolph crushed the root into a white paste using an old-fashioned mortar and pestle.

"Remember what I called this?" he said, gesturing to the root.

"Was it shookum?"

"Skookum," Randolph said. "It means very, very strong."

"It's just a root," Jesse said.

Randolph took Jesse's hand and folded back all the fingers except one. Then he took that one finger and touched it to the paste. Jesse touched his finger to the tip of his tongue. A second later he tasted something tart in his mouth. He'd never tasted anything like it before.

"Hey!" He gasped, backing up. "I can taste it!"

Randolph just nodded. Suddenly Jesse realized why he'd done that.

"That stuff's pretty strong," he said.

Randolph started grinding the root again and adding the other ingredients.

"When we're done with this it'll be even stronger," he said. "Our medicine is one that you have to be very sick to use. If you're not sick, it's so strong it will kill you."

It wasn't long before Randolph was finished. Using the alder stick, he scraped the grainy whitish paste out of the pestle and into a hand-carved wooden bowl. Then, they headed for the dock. The three whales swam over to meet them.

They climbed into the small rubber raft Jesse had used the day before and they started to row out into the cove, the whales trailing along behind. It was evening now and the air was still. The surface of the water was like glass. As they got farther away from the emergency center, the only sound Jesse heard was the dip and splash of the oars. It seemed as if the whole world had suddenly become quiet, waiting for this solemn moment when the Haida medicine would be administered.

Now Jesse could hear another sound — the labored wheezing and gurgling of a sick whale. Not far away, Luna floated. Jesse had just begun to wonder where Willy had gone when the whale suddenly surfaced right next to the raft and stared right at Jesse as if asking what he planned to do now.

Jesse locked eyes with his friend, trying to telegraph the importance of the moment. The other medicine hadn't worked. This was their last chance. Randolph nodded at Jesse. Jesse gave Willy the sign to open his mouth.

Willy opened his mouth. A few feet away, Luna

did the same. Jesse picked up the wooden bowl and held it for Randolph, who scooped up the grainy white paste with a large leaf. Slowly, carefully, he began to apply the paste to Luna's tongue. Jesse almost winced at the thought of the taste, but he knew these were very smart creatures. Somehow they understood that this was a good thing.

Randolph scooped more of the paste out of the bowl. He'd developed a rhythm to it. As if it wasn't only *what* he was giving Luna, but *how* he was giving it as well. The older man slowly closed his eyes and began to sing a soft song.

With one hand, Jesse reached out and stroked Willy to reassure him. Surely this song was part of the medicine. It was a healing song.

"It's going to be okay, Willy," Jesse whispered. "Luna's going to be okay. The medicine's going to work."

Jesse kept stroking Willy, and Randolph kept singing. The song filled the silence until it almost seemed as if there were others joining in. Jesse could imagine a place in the woods, a Haida village where Randolph's tribesmen squatted near a fire, joining in the song, offering their spiritual support.

Jesse looked at Willy and saw a big drop of water at the corner of the orca's eye.

"Randolph?" Jesse asked in a whisper.

"Yes, Jesse?" Randolph replied, still humming the healing song.

"Can a whale cry?"

Randolph looked over at Willy. Of course, Willy was in the water and all wet anyway. Maybe it was all just Jesse's imagination.

"It's probably just sea water, Jesse," Randolph said.

"Yeah." Jesse nodded. "You're probably right."

But he only said that for Randolph's sake. Or maybe it was Willy's sake. Because Jesse knew the whale, and knew what he was feeling. Jesse felt a pang deep in his heart. Willy was stuck here in this cove with his sick sister. And somewhere out there in the straits, Catspaw was searching for them, calling for them, crying for them. And Jesse knew the feeling. He'd known it all his life. To be missing someone, to want them and not be able to get to them . . . .

Behind him Randolph sang the healing song. By now Jesse was familiar enough with it to hum along. And then, the most amazing thing happened. Willy began to whistle it. Jesse turned and gave Randolph a shocked look, but the older man only nodded knowingly. Now Littlespot rose in the water beside his big brother and he began to sing, as if all their voices together would somehow add strength to the medicine.

And then, finally, another voice joined in, weak and faint. It was Luna.

It was very dark. Jesse and Randolph paddled slowly back toward the dock. Way up on the beach, the emergency tent was aglow with lights and buzzing with activity, but out on the water it was still calm and quiet.

They reached the dock and climbed up. Jesse looked back out into the dark, looking for Luna but unable now to see her. He felt Randolph's arm go around his shoulder.

"We've done everything in our power to help," Randolph said. "All we can do now is let them sleep."

"Wait and see if the spirits are with us?" Jesse asked.

"The spirits are always with us," Randolph said. "But tonight, we also need some luck."

Randolph started to turn, but Jesse didn't.

"You coming?"

"In a little while," Jesse said.

"Okay." Randolph started down the dock. Jesse sat down at the dock's edge. Willy surfaced close by. It was funny how Jesse knew that Willy would be there. Jesse bent down and spoke softly to him.

"I'll make a deal with you," he said, thinking of the conversation he'd had with Nadine earlier that afternoon. "You help Luna feel better. You lead your brother and sister out of this cove. You find your mother. You do that, and I'll do everything I can to keep your water clean and safe for as long as I live. Okay?"

Willy blinked. Then he raised one of his flukes and waved it within Jesse's reach. Jesse took hold of the end of the fluke and shook it.

"Then it's a deal," he said. "I'm taking you at your word. And I'm holding you to it."

18

The campsite was empty when Jesse returned to it that night. He knew Annie and Glen were still out looking for Elvis. What a little jerk the kid was, running away just when everyone should have been trying to help Willy and his brother and sister. But somehow Jesse also understood. He could see how he might have done the same thing when he was that age. He just hoped that wherever Elvis was, he was okay.

He was up at the crack of dawn. Elvis's sleeping bag was empty. He couldn't imagine where the kid had spent the night. In the woods? In jail? Jesse quickly got dressed. He couldn't do anything about Elvis right now, but he could go see what was going on with Luna.

He hurried down through the woods to the emergency tent. Just as he got there, he noticed that Dr. Haley was standing at the end of the dock, looking out at the cove. Randolph was walking out toward her. Jesse quickly followed. As he got closer, he could see Willy circling out in the cove with Littlespot right behind. And a third whale splashed between them. Could it be?

Yes! It was Luna!

Dr. Haley looked back at Randolph as he joined her on the dock.

"How's it going?" he asked, but he had a smile on his face because he already knew.

Dr. Haley also smiled. "Looks like Luna's getting better."

"My medicine is very powerful," Randolph said, crossing his arms.

Dr. Haley raised an eyebrow. "*Your* medicine?"

"Did I say that?" Randolph grinned. "I mean, your medicine."

Dr. Haley smiled back. "I don't know what you did, Randolph. But whatever it was, I'm glad you did it."

"So am I," Jesse said, joining them.

Randolph put his arm around Jesse's shoulder. "Let's just call it a group effort."

They turned and headed back down the dock toward the emergency tent.

"Is it time to get them back to Catspaw?" Jesse asked.

"Yes," said Dr. Haley. "I just want to check on the currents. The last thing we want to do is lead them back into the oil spill."

They went into the tent. Milner, the man from

the oil company, was there again. He turned to a man Jesse had never seen before. The man was balding, with a ruddy complexion. He was heavy and had a large belly protruding over the buckle of his belt.

"How's the containment going, Wilcox?" Milner asked.

"The slick will reach the cove pretty soon," Wilcox replied. "In a few hours I'm sealing off the cove with a boom to keep the oil slick out. We'll put out nets to keep the whales in. By that time, even if the whales could leave, they'd be swimming right into the slick."

"Then I'm going out on the water now, to try and lead them to the open sea," Dr. Haley said.

It sounded like the right thing to Jesse, but he noticed Milner and Wilcox shared an apprehensive glance. Then Milner took Dr. Haley aside. "Listen, Kate," he said. "I know you're going to be successful. I know you'll get them out of here before the oil comes. But if you don't, we need a plan."

Dr. Haley eyed him suspiciously. "And you have one in mind."

Jesse was dying to hear what that plan was, but Milner led Dr. Haley away and talked in a whisper to her. Jesse watched their faces. He knew Milner sounded earnest and honest, but deep down he didn't trust him. He could tell from

Dr. Haley's face that she didn't trust him completely either.

When they finished talking, Dr. Haley came toward Jesse. "Come on, you're coming with me."

"What'd he say?" Jesse asked.

"It's not important," Dr. Haley replied. "What's important is that we get those whales out of the cove before the oil gets here."

They went out onto the dock and got into the *Zodiac*. Jesse got into the front and they headed toward the whales. When they got close to Willy, Jesse leaned over the rail toward him.

"This is it, Willy," he shouted. "We've got to get you out of here now. You've got to make Luna leave. Okay?"

Jesse looked back at Dr. Haley and nodded. The *Zodiac* turned and headed toward the straits. Jesse scampered to the back of the boat and waved his arms.

"Come on, Willy! This way!"

Willy started to follow the boat, and Littlespot started to follow Willy. Luna brought up the rear, but she moved slowly. Just as they got to the mouth of the cove, she dove and disappeared from sight. Jesse gave Dr. Haley a worried look.

Luna came up again.

"Let's go, Luna!" Jesse shouted. "How about a little sibling rivalry here? Your brothers are whipping your butt!"

Luna seemed to give it a little more effort. Jesse looked around and saw that they were almost out of the cove now.

"Just a little farther and we're home free." Dr. Haley crossed her fingers.

Suddenly the three whales spouted and dove at once, disappearing beneath the waves. The driver of the *Zodiac* cut his engine. Jesse stared at the water for a sign of them, but saw nothing.

"Where are they?" he asked.

"Maybe they're past us," Dr. Haley said. "Underwater, heading out to the open sea."

But Jesse had a bad feeling and looked back. His hopes for their freedom fell. The whales had surfaced again — back in the cove.

19

The hope in Dr. Haley's face vanished. The *Zodiac* slowed and turned around. Jesse stood in the bow and watched. Once again, Luna floated listlessly in the middle of the cove. She must have been exhausted. The oil sickness must have weakened her more than they'd thought. Willy and Littlespot were swimming in restless circles around her.

Jesse caught Dr. Haley's eye.

"We'll try again," she said.

But Jesse shook his head. "No. Luna's not ready."

Dr. Haley studied his face for a moment, then nodded as if she knew he were right. They headed back toward the dock. Nadine and Randolph were waiting there for them. John Milner and a bunch of other people passed them, heading for the end of the dock. Randolph looked disappointed.

"Luna must not have the strength," Jesse tried to explain.

"It's not just that," Randolph said. "They've given the order to boom off the cove, seal it completely to keep out the oil, and protect the whales."

Out in the cove, two large white fishing boats were laying down the long yellow boom while two smaller gray boats were putting out a net attached to white floats.

"Protect them?" Nadine gave him a withering look. "Don't you mean *trap* them? It's not just the boom. They're putting down nets, too."

"The nets are for the whale's protection," Dr. Haley explained. "An hour from now, if they were allowed to swim under the boom and out of the cove, they'd be swimming right into a massive oil slick. They'd die."

"But if they're trapped in the cove they'll never get back to their pod," Jesse argued. "They'll never get back to their family."

It was clear that Dr. Haley already knew that. She nodded. "You saw what happened when we tried to lead them out of the cove. They wouldn't leave. Luna's not ready. This is the best we can do."

But anger and frustration were building in Jesse. The thought of Willy, Luna, and Littlespot never seeing Catspaw again set him off.

"No, it's not the best you can do!" he yelled. "Not hurting them in the first place would have been the best! Not ruining their home would have been the best! This is just a bunch of bull!"

"But Jesse—" Dr. Haley started to say.

Jesse didn't hang around to listen to any more of her stupid explanations. He'd had it with these adults and their dumb excuses. He stormed away down the dock, not sure where he was going, but certain that he didn't want to hear what they had to say.

As he passed the emergency tent the sound of a television caught his attention. A bunch of emergency workers were crowded around a small portable TV. On the black-and-white screen was Milner, that guy from the oil company. He was being interviewed in a studio somewhere. Since Milner was now out on the dock, Jesse knew the interview must have been taped earlier.

"We at Benbrook Oil are pleased to announce we have arranged for the whales to be lifted out of the cove this afternoon and taken to a marine rescue center where they can be properly cared for while they recuperate," he was saying.

Suddenly the interview on the TV went off. A harried-looking news reporter came on. He was pressing an earplug into his ear. He appeared to be standing on a cliff overlooking a body of water. Behind him a fire was raging. . . . A fire on the *water!*

"This is Ken Rogers with Channel Seven Eyewitness News," the reporter said hastily. "We're coming to you live from a bluff near Lawson Reef, the sight of the *Dakar* oil spill disaster a few days ago. As you can see behind me, a new and devastating development has just taken place. According to our sources, a crew attempting to repair the ship a few hours ago accidentally ignited fuel vapors, causing an explosion. We've now learned that the oil slick itself is on fire. In a related development, all residents inhabiting the islands in and around Haro Strait are being asked to evacuate at this time."

Jesse and Nadine stared at each other with wide eyes.

"Evacuate?" Jesse said, amazed.

"They'll have to get the whales out first," Nadine said.

They both turned and looked back out at the cove. The white-hulled fishing boats were out there, trying to herd the whales together. One of the boats had a large hoist with a sling to lift the whales out of the water. Out in the distance over the straits, they could see a cloud of dark gray smoke — from the burning oil.

Someone was tugging at Jesse's shirt. He turned around and found Elvis standing behind him.

"Where the heck have you been?" Jesse asked.

"Saving your blubbery butt," Elvis replied.

Jesse made a face. "What are you talking about?"

"I'll tell you, but you have to trust me," Elvis said.

"Why should I trust *you*?" Jesse asked.

"Because nobody ever has," Elvis said.

Jesse studied the kid's face. He was completely serious. For once he was telling the truth.

"Come with me," Elvis said. He started to jog back onto the pier. Jesse and Nadine followed. Elvis stopped about halfway out on the dock.

"You see that guy?" Elvis pointed at Milner, standing on the end of the dock, watching the rescue effort.

"Yeah, he's the guy from the oil company," Jesse said.

"Right," said Elvis. Then he pointed out at one of the fishing boats in the cove. Wilcox, the heavy-set man, was standing on the deck of the boat, directing the people who were trying to save the whales. "See that guy?"

"Yeah."

"His name's Wilcox," Elvis said.

"I know. So?"

"So about an hour ago I was sitting in a donut shop in town," Elvis said. "Like waiting for the next ferry to get me off this stupid island, and guess who sat down in a booth behind me?"

"Who?" Jesse asked, getting a little annoyed.

"Those two guys," Elvis said. "Milner and Wilcox. And Wilcox starts talking about how he hasn't taken an orca out of the wild in twenty years."

"That's right," said Nadine. "They're not allowed to anymore."

"Except Wilcox says he's got three right in his hands," Elvis said.

Jesse and Nadine gave each other another look. It was obvious which three whales Wilcox was talking about.

"Wilcox offered Milner a million dollars each for Luna and Littlespot, and two million dollars for Willy because he's already trained," Elvis said. "He said the males are good because they can breed them and he said Willy was a gold mine."

It sounded like an outrageous lie, but Jesse had a feeling the kid was telling the truth. "What did Milner say to all this?"

"He said Wilcox had to be careful to make it look like he had the whale's best interests at heart," Elvis said. "Then Wilcox said he did. He said the whales were really sick and they would need long term rehabilitation."

"Wait a minute," Nadine said. "This doesn't make any sense. First you tell us Wilcox offered Milner four million dollars for the whales. Then you tell us he's paying all that money just to rehabilitate them?"

"He wants to rehabilitate them," Elvis said. "But he also plans to charge people money to see them. He's gonna put them in the kind of place

Willy used to be in. When he said long term, he meant *really* long term."

Jesse grit his teeth and made a fist. "I knew it! I knew this was all too good to be true. The only reason they're saving those whales is to sell them into captivity. They'll never get back to their family."

The next thing Jesse knew, he was running down the dock as fast as his legs could carry him.

20

By the time Jesse reached the end of the dock, the guys on the boats had gotten Littlespot into the sling. The small whale was whistling and crying out in fear. Willy was floating nearby watching. Milner was standing with Randolph and Dr. Haley. Jesse stormed up to him. Elvis and Nadine were right behind.

"You're a liar!" he shouted. "You're not trying to help these whales! You're selling them to an aquarium!"

"Jesse, stop." Dr. Haley stepped between them. "I assure you that they'll be returned to their natural habitat as soon as they're ready."

Elvis pointed at Wilcox out on the fishing boat. "Not if he has anything to do with it!"

"What are you talking about?" Randolph asked.

"You're going to lock 'em up and throw away the key!" Jesse yelled.

Dr. Haley and Randolph both gave Milner questioning looks.

"I'm afraid you kids are going to have to leave," Milner said, nodding at some of his assistants.

Jesse could see they were going to get herded away. He darted around Dr. Haley and came face to face with this man from the oil company.

"You promised you'd try to get them back to their mother!" Jesse shouted. "You're not going to get away with this!" He gave Milner a push.

Splash! The man from the oil company fell off the dock and into the water.

"Jesse!" Dr. Haley gasped, stunned. But Jesse noticed a smile come over Randolph's face.

As one of Milner's assistants moved to help him, Elvis pushed *him* into the water, too.

"Get 'em, Willy!" Jesse shouted, signaling Willy toward the boat that had Littlespot.

Willy instantly dove. Wilcox and the men in his boat pressed toward the rails, searching the water for him.

Ker-splash! The next thing Jesse knew, the boat rose into the air and flipped, spilling the men into the water. Willy had tipped it over with his tail! Littlespot slid out of the sling and was free again! The men came to the surface, spitting water and gasping for breath.

In the commotion that followed, Jesse grabbed Elvis and whispered something to him. Elvis nodded and ran off. Meanwhile, Jesse and Nadine went down the dock to the *Little Dipper*, Glen's boat.

Jesse jumped off the dock and landed in the boat. He quickly started to untie the lines. Nadine stayed on the dock.

"What are you doing?" she gasped.

"Hop in," Jesse said.

"You know how to drive this thing by yourself?" Nadine asked uncertainly.

"Don't worry about it," Jesse said. "Just get in!"

Nadine didn't budge. "Where did Elvis go?"

"He's going to take care of something for me," Jesse said, flicking the ignition switch. "You coming or not?"

Varrroooomm! The engines roared to life and Jesse began to pull away from the dock. At the very last second, Nadine hopped on board. Jesse steered toward the swim platform where Elvis was waiting. Jesse pulled the boat up to the platform.

"All set?" he asked.

"Yeah." Elvis hopped on board. "Let's get out of here!"

Jesse gunned the engine and headed toward the boom blocking the entrance to the cove. Nadine and Elvis held on to the console.

"You know how to drive this thing?" Elvis yelled.

"Not really," Jesse yelled back. As the boat neared the boom, Jesse pulled back on the throttle and let it idle. "Willy!" he shouted.

Willy surfaced near the boat. Littlespot came up next to him and Luna trailed behind. On the dock, some men were pulling Wilcox from the water. Wilcox was shouting something about getting the kids. Jesse reached over the side of the boat and rubbed Willy on the snout.

"We're getting out of here, okay," Jesse said. "Now pay attention. Here's one from the old days."

He gave Willy the signal to jump. Willy nodded and chattered.

"You remember?" Jesse grinned. "Great. Let's give 'em a show!"

Willy dove beneath the surface. For a second everything was quiet.

"What did that signal mean?" Nadine asked.

"You'll see." Jesse got behind the wheel of the *Little Dipper* again and gunned the engine. This time he steered straight toward the boom.

"You can't crash into it!" Elvis yelled. "We'll never get through!"

But Jesse held the throttle down and aimed for the center of the boom. They were closing in on the boom fast. Forty yards, thirty . . . twenty . . .

Suddenly the water in front of the boat parted and a huge black and white torpedo burst into the air. It was Willy, filling the air like a blimp.

Crash! Willy hit the boom with a tremendous splash. The boom collapsed, leaving a gaping hole.

Jesse steered right through it, then quickly turned and cut the motor.

"What about Luna?" Nadine asked.

Jesse nodded back toward the cove. Willy and Littlespot were nudging their tired sister through the hole in the boom. Some of the people back on the dock were cheering and clapping, but Wilcox's men were running toward another boat.

"They're coming after us!" Nadine cried.

"Guess again," Elvis said with a devilish look.

Wilcox's men jumped on the boat and sped away from the dock. Little did they know that Elvis had tied the anchor line to the dock.

Sproing! The anchor line pulled tight and the boat slammed to a stop.

Ker-splash! Carried by momentum, Wilcox and his men flipped forward into the water again!

"All right!" Elvis shouted.

"Look!" Nadine shouted and pointed ahead. Willy and his brother and sister were heading out into the strait, spouting and diving and calling.

Jesse turned the boat around and started to follow. He wanted to make sure the whales got safely out of the cove and into the open sea.

21

"Where're the whales?" Jesse shouted to Elvis, who was in the bow.

"I don't see 'em!" Elvis shouted back. "They must be under the water."

They were in the drifting smoke now. Nadine looked scared.

"Jesse!" she yelled. "We have to go back!"

"Not until I make sure they get past the oil," Jesse replied.

Meanwhile, the smoke was growing thicker. Jesse coughed. He looked around and realized he couldn't see San Juan Island anymore. He felt a hand go around his forearm. It was Nadine.

"Jesse," she said. "I'm scared."

"Me, too," Jesse said.

Up in the bow, Elvis leaned over the side and dipped his hand in the water. When he brought it up, Jesse could see that it was black with oil.

"I think we're in trouble," Elvis yelled, wiping his hand on his shirt.

"Any sign of the whales?" Jesse shouted back.

"I don't see anything except smoke," Nadine said, and coughed. "Jesse, we have to turn around."

"Okay, just tell me which way is around," Jesse said.

"Oh, no," Nadine gasped. "I can't tell!"

"Hey, you guys," Elvis called from the bow.

"What?" Jesse asked.

"I see something in the water."

"Whales?" Nadine asked hopefully.

"No, more like — "

Crunk! The *Little Dipper* suddenly shuddered, throwing everyone forward. The boat came to a stop.

"Rocks." Elvis finished the sentence.

They could hear the sound of water rushing in somewhere below the water line. The *Little Dipper* began to list to one side. Although Jesse had never spent much time on boats, he knew what it meant. They were sinking!

Elvis looked really scared. "If you get me out of this, I swear I'll never touch your stuff or cross the line or say bad things about you ever again."

"Promise?" Jesse asked.

Elvis nodded.

"I'm not going to let anything happen to you," Jesse said.

Nadine coughed. Elvis coughed. The smoke was growing thicker and thicker.

"Hey, you feel something?" Elvis asked.

Jesse stood still. Oh, no, it was heat!

"The fire must be getting close!" Elvis shouted.

Thump-a-thump-a-thump-a. Now they heard another, more distant sound gradually growing louder.

"A helicopter!" Jesse shouted.

"Hey! We're down here!" Everyone started to wave and yell up through the smoke. Meanwhile, the *Little Dipper* slid off the rocks and began to roll with the waves. The water in the boat was knee deep.

From the helicopter above came a rescue harness on a cable. Jesse reached up and grabbed it. He and Nadine locked eyes.

"Jesse — " she gasped.

"I know!" Jesse shouted back. "There's only room for one!"

"You go!" Nadine said.

"No way!" Jesse shouted back. He helped Elvis into the harness.

"Pull it up!" he shouted up to the helicopter. "Pull it up!"

The harness started to rise. Suddenly Jesse realized he was sweating. It was the heat from the fire. He couldn't see it through the smoke, but it had to be close.

"You're the best brother I ever had!" Elvis called to him from above as the harness rose.

"I'm the *only* brother you ever had," Jesse yelled back.

The harness rose higher. Elvis looked white with fear.

"I'm scared!" he whimpered.

"Don't worry, kid!" Jesse shouted at him. "It's just like bungee jumping."

"I never went bungee jumping!" Elvis shouted back. "I lied!"

No kidding, Jesse thought. A second later, the harness disappeared into the smoke above. The harness came back down, empty, and Jesse sent Nadine up. Then, he waited for his turn. Meanwhile, it was getting hotter. Jesse felt like he was standing next to the campfire. The boat was practically underwater now. Jesse squinted up through the smoke. Where was the harness?

Suddenly he saw something, but it wasn't the harness. It was the flames! They were coming toward him, traveling over the oily water. Jesse had to shield his eyes with his hands. The heat and smoke were so great he couldn't stand it!

Where was that harness?

Suddenly it dropped down through the smoke. Jesse grabbed it. His hands were covered with oil, but he thought he could climb in. The flames were just a few feet away. It was so hot that he couldn't breathe!

"Go!" he screamed.

"Are you secure?" a voice from the helicopter shouted back.

He was covered with oil. The flames were going to be on him any second.

"I'm on!" Jesse screamed, holding on for dear life. "Just go! *Go!*"

Suddenly he felt himself lift from the boat. He was only about one-third into the harness. He kept trying to pull himself all the way in, but his oily hands were too slippery!

The harness was rising. If he could just hold on!

His hands were slipping!

Above him the smoke cleared. He could see the helicopter. He could see one of the crewmen reaching toward him. He could see Nadine's face, her eyes wide and frightened.

Jesse slid back. Now he was holding on by his fingertips!

Only a few feet more to the helicopter.

"Hold on!" Elvis shouted.

Jesse tried to hold on for all his might.

"I'm slipping!" he yelled.

"Take my hand!" shouted the crewman.

Jesse reached for it and let go of the harness.

He tried to grab the crewman's hand, but before he could, he slipped and fell.

22

He was falling back into the smoke and flames.

WHAP! He hit the water so hard it stunned him.

Then he was under. The water felt cool, even refreshing. He opened his eyes and looked up. It was like looking at clouds and sky. The dark clouds were the patches of burning oil. They had orange and crimson edges. The blue patches must've been uncovered water.

He swam up and broke the surface in a blue patch. He gasped for breath. The air came into his lungs hot like a steam bath.

"Help!" he gasped.

The flames were too hot. He could feel them scorching his face. He took another breath and dove under.

He was underwater again. How long could he last? Looking up from under the surface it was mostly black clouds above. He couldn't find a spot with enough blue to go up and get another breath!

His lungs were starting to burn for air. He felt bubbles start to dribble from his lips. Oh, no! Oh, no!

A shadowy form was moving toward him. At first Jesse didn't understand. Then he realized . . .

It was Willy!

The whale slowed down and passed close to him. His big whale eye looked at Jesse and blinked. Jesse grabbed his dorsal fin and Willy shot forward.

They came up in a blue patch and Jesse gasped for air and held onto Willy's curled dorsal fin. But they were surrounded by flames. They couldn't stay.

There was no place to go.

Except down.

"Go for it, Willy!" Jesse shouted. "Go for it!"

He took a deep breath and held his nose with one hand. They shot back down into the water, racing faster than Jesse had ever gone underwater. He could barely hold on!

Where was Willy going?

What did it matter?

The sea was covered with flames.

Jesse felt his lungs start to burn again. He was going to have to let go.

Then a big shadow appeared in the water ahead of them. . . . A boat!

The water around it was blue!

Jesse popped up to the surface on Willy's back and took a delirious breath. He was so weak he could hardly hang on to Willy.

"Jesse!" someone screamed.

Jesse twisted his head around. It was Annie! And Glen! And Randolph! Then the boat must've been the *Natselane*!

Hands reached down and grabbed him under the arms, pulling him off Willy's back. Jesse felt himself lifted out of the water and pulled on board. He looked back down into the water and saw a familiar sight — Willy lolling nearby.

"You saved his life, Willy," Annie said.

It was true. Jesse grinned and felt the sea water drain out of his hair and down his face. He waved at the killer whale. "Thanks, Willy."

23

They'd just wrapped Jesse in a blanket when the helicopter appeared and hovered over the deck of the *Natselane.*

"We need to find some more people," a crewman shouted down. "Can you take these two?"

Nadine and Elvis stuck their heads out of the bay behind the cockpit.

"Yeah we'll take 'em!" Glen shouted back.

Nadine and Elvis climbed off the rescue boat and were lowered down to the deck. As soon as they got out, the crewmen drove the boat away.

"I thought we lost you!" Nadine cried and threw her arms around Jesse. She hugged him as hard as she could.

Meanwhile, Elvis stood before Glen and Annie, looking sheepish. "You don't have to say it. I know I shouldn't have run away. In fact, I ground my-self."

Annie kneeled down and hugged him. "And I'm

sorry I broke my promise. It'll never happen again."

Randolph had climbed up into the cockpit and was steering the boat away. "Catspaw!" he shouted.

Jesse quickly looked up. "Where?"

Randolph pointed ahead, out where the water was still blue and uncovered by oil. Jesse and the others peered out and saw Catspaw and the other members of the pod. Jesse went to the side of the boat and leaned toward Willy.

"You did it, boy," he said. "You found her."

Jesse expected Willy to swim off, but the whale stayed beside the *Natselane*.

"Go on," Jesse urged him. "You have to go. You'll be with your family again."

Willy let out a soft, sad whistle. Jesse knew what he was saying. He could feel tears welling up in his eyes.

"I don't want you to go either," he said. "But you have to. You have the best thing anybody could ever ask for. You have your family. You have your mom."

Willy let out a little cry. Glen came up beside Jesse.

"He won't leave," Glen said.

"What's he waiting for?" Jesse asked.

Now Randolph joined them. "He's waiting for you to give him the signal."

He was right. Jesse bit his lip. Once he sent

Willy away, he might never see him again. But he had to do it. He *had* to! Jesse could feel the tears stream down his eyes as he pointed toward the pod ahead of them.

"I love you, Willy," he gasped. Then he gave the signal to go.

Willy's great eye blinked. He swam off to the side, dove, and then leapt high into the air, spinning slowly, flapping his flukes at Jesse.

Jesse closed his eyes and felt Glen's arms go around him. Annie's arms went around him, too.

The *Natselane* slowed. Jesse opened his eyes. The pod of whales had gathered together. They were spyhopping, chattering happily, rubbing up against each other as if welcoming Willy and his brother and sister home.

24

Jesse and Nadine stood on the bow of the *Natselane* as it headed back to the island. The fresh wind was in their faces. The sky ahead was clear blue. The smoke and fire were behind them.

Nadine squeezed Jesse's hand. "You could come back next summer. When Willy's pod returns."

Next summer? Jesse turned and looked at her. "Can't we do something before that?"

Nadine smiled. "You mean, without Willy?"

Jesse nodded and leaned toward her. Hopefully no one else was watching.

Just then Elvis appeared and stood before them.

"What are you looking at?" Jesse asked.

"What are *you* looking at?" Elvis shot back. Then he reached into his pocket and handed a creased, dog-eared photograph to Jesse. Jesse looked down at it and felt his eyes widen. His whole body tingled and goose bumps ran down his arms.

"It's for you," Elvis said. "It's why I hated your guts."

Jesse stared down at the photo of himself and his mother. He was just a little kid, maybe four years old, when it was taken. Both he and his mother were grinning. They looked happy. For that moment, at least, they must have *been* happy.

The photo had been ripped in half, right down the middle, splitting Jesse from his mom. But the pieces had been taped together again.

"It's the only picture I ever had of her," Elvis said. "And *you* had to be in it. It kind of had an accident. But I taped it back together."

Jesse looked at his half brother. Now he knew for sure that under that wise guy know-it-all exterior was a good kid. A kid who'd been hurt just as he had, but a kid who was trying to deal with it and not let it get the best of him.

"Thanks, Elvis," Jesse said. And he really meant it.

Elvis looked off toward the island and then back at Jesse. "There's one more thing," he said. "Remember how I said she never talked about you?"

Jesse nodded.

"Well, she talked about you all the time," Elvis said. "She never stopped talking about you. She really missed you, Jesse. She really felt bad about what happened."

The words made Jesse feel light-headed. He'd always wondered. He'd always *wished* . . . but now he knew. She'd cared. She'd felt bad about what happened.

"She loved you," Elvis said.

Jesse didn't even think about what he did next. He just reached for the kid and hugged him.

Annie and Glen came out on the foredeck.

"So what do you think?" Annie asked her husband.

"I guess we can keep him," Glen replied. "I mean, I would hate to break up the set."

Jesse let go of Elvis and they both looked at Annie and Glen. Both of them had red-rimmed eyes.

"So what do you say, Elvis?" Glen asked. "You want to stay with us? Be part of the family?"

Elvis pressed a finger against his lower lip. "Uh, can I get back to you on that?"

"No," Glen said. "This offer expires immediately."

"Hey, I was just kidding," Elvis said. "Just kidding. This has been the coolest vacation I've ever been on!"

Annie gave him a look. "Oh, come on, Elvis, I bet you always say that."

"No, honest, I'm telling the truth," Elvis said. Then he looked a little sheepish and added, "For once."

They all laughed. Jesse put his arm around Nadine's shoulder and squeezed her. This was his family now. And it was the best he'd ever had.

ABOUT THE AUTHOR

Todd Strasser has written many award-winning novels for young and teenage readers. Among his best known books are *Help! I'm Trapped in My Teacher's Body* and *Help! I'm Trapped in the First Day of School.* He speaks frequently at schools about the craft of writing and conducts writing workshops for young people.